D1029642

Ship Island and Other Stories

LAWRENCE MEMORIAL PUBLIC LIBRARY
WINDSOR, NORTH CAROLINA

ELIZABETH SPENCER

NO LONGER THE
PROPERTY OF

Ship Island
and
Other Stories

McGRAW-HILL BOOK COMPANY

New York   Toronto   London   Sydney

ALBEMARLE REGIONAL LIBRARY
WINTON, N. C.

SHIP ISLAND AND OTHER STORIES

Copyright © 1968 by Elizabeth Spencer. All Rights Reserved.
Printed in the United States of America. No part of this publica-
tion may be reproduced, stored in a retrieval system, or transmitted,
in any form or by any means, electronic, mechanical, photocopy-
ing, recording, or otherwise, without the prior written permission
of the publisher.

Library of Congress Catalog Card Number: 68-22767
First Edition   60182

"First Dark," first printed in *The New Yorker*, © 1959, by The
New Yorker Magazine, Inc., in the United States and Canada. All
Rights Reserved.
"The Fishing Lake," first printed in *The New Yorker*, © 1964,
by the New Yorker Magazine, Inc., in the United States and
Canada. All Rights Reserved.
"The Little Brown Girl," first printed in *The New Yorker*,
copyright 1957, by The New Yorker Magazine, Inc., in the United
States and Canada. All Rights Reserved.
"A Southern Landscape," first printed in *The New Yorker*, ©
1960, by The New Yorker Magazine, Inc., in the United States
and Canada. All Rights Reserved.
"Ship Island," first printed in *The New Yorker*, © 1964, by
The New Yorker Magazine, Inc., in the United States and Canada.
All Rights Reserved.
"The Visit," first printed in *Prairie Schooner*, copyright © 1964,
University of Nebraska Press. All Rights Reserved.
"The White Azalea," first printed in *The Texas Quarterly*,
copyright 1961 by The University of Texas.

"First Dark" and "Ship Island" were awarded the O. Henry
Prize Stories awards for the years 1960 and 1966.
"The Visit" was selected as one of the "Best American Short
Stories" in the Martha Foley Collection, 1965.

To Eudora Welty

Contents

Ship Island and Other Stories

First Dark

When Tom Beavers started coming back to Richton, Mississippi, on weekends, after the war was over, everybody in town was surprised and pleased. They had never noticed him much before he paid them this compliment; now they could not say enough nice things. There was not much left in Richton for him to call family—just his aunt who had raised him, Miss Rita Beavers, old as God, ugly as sin, deaf as a post. So he must be fond of the town, they reasoned; certainly it was a pretty old place. Far too many young men had left it and never come back at all.

He would drive in every Friday night from Jackson, where he worked. All weekend, his Ford, dusty of flank, like a hard-ridden horse, would sit parked down the hill near Miss Rita's old wire front gate, which sagged from the top hinge and had worn a span in the ground. On Saturday morning, he would head for the drugstore, then the post office; then he would be observed walking here and there around the streets under the shade trees. It was as though he were looking for something.

He wore steel taps on his heels, and in the still the click of them on the sidewalks would sound across the big front lawns and all the way up to the porches of the houses, where two ladies might be sitting behind a row of ferns. They would identify him to one another, murmuring in their fine little voices, and say it was just too bad there was nothing here for young people. It was just a shame they didn't have one or two more old houses here, for a Pilgrimage—look how Natchez had waked up.

On Saturday morning in early October, Tom Beavers sat at the counter in the drugstore and reminded Totsie Poteet, the drugstore clerk, of a ghost story. Did he remember the strange old man who used to appear to people who were coming into Richton along the Jackson road at twilight—what they called "first dark"?

"Sure I remember," said Totsie. "Old Cud'n Jimmy Wiltshire used to tell us about him every time we went possum hunting. I could see him plain as I can see you, the way he used to tell it. Tall, with a top hat on, yeah, and waiting in the weeds alongside the road ditch, so'n you couldn't tell if he wasn't taller than any mortal man could be, because you couldn't tell if he was standing down in the ditch or not. It would look like he just grew up out of the weeds. Then he'd signal to you."

"Them that stopped never saw anybody," said Tom Beavers, stirring his coffee. "There were lots of folks besides Mr. Jimmy that saw him."

"There was, let me see . . ." Totsie enumerated others—some men, some women, some known to drink, others who never touched a drop. There was no way to explain it. "There was that story the road gang told. Do you remember, or were you off at school? It was while they were straightening the road out to the highway—taking the curves out and building a new bridge. Anyway, they said that one night at quitting time, along in the winter and just about dark, this old guy signalled to some of 'em. They said they went over and he asked them to move a bulldozer they had left across the road, because he had a wagon back behind on a little dirt road, with a sick nigger girl in it. Had to get to the doctor and this was the only way. They claimed they knew didn't nobody live back there on that little old road, but niggers can come from anywhere. So they moved the bulldozer and cleared back a whole lot of other stuff, and waited and waited. Not only didn't no wagon ever come, but the man that had stopped them, he was gone, too. They was right shook up over it. You never heard that one?"

"No, I never did." Tom Beavers said this with his eyes looking up over his coffee cup, as though he sat behind a hand of cards. His lashes and brows were heavier than was ordinary, and worked as a veil might, to keep you away from knowing exactly what he was thinking.

"They said he was tall and had a hat on." The screen door flapped to announce a customer, but Totsie kept on talking. "But whether he was a white man or a real light-colored nigger they couldn't say. Some said one and some said another. I figured they'd been pulling on the jug a little earlier than usual. You know why? I never heard of *our* ghost *saying* nothing. Did you, Tom?"

He moved away on the last words, the way a clerk will, talking back over his shoulder and ahead of him to his new customer at the same time, as though he had two voices and two heads. "And what'll it be today, Miss Frances?"

The young woman standing at the counter had a pre-scription already out of her bag. She stood with it poised between her fingers, but her attention was drawn toward Tom Beavers, his coffee cup, and the conversation she had interrupted. She was a girl whom no ordinary description would fit. One would have to know first of all who she was: Frances Harvey. After that, it was all right for her to be a little odd-looking, with her reddish hair that curled back from her brow, her light eyes, and her high, pale temples. This is not the material for being pretty, but in Frances Harvey it was what could sometimes be beauty. Her family home was laden with history that nobody but the Harveys could remember. It would have been on a Pilgrimage if Richton had had one. Frances still lived in it, looking after an invalid mother.

"What were you-all talking about?" she wanted to know.

"About that ghost they used to tell about," said Totsie, holding out his hand for the prescription. "The one people used to see just outside of town, on the Jackson road."

"But why?" she demanded. "Why were you talking about him?"

"Tom, here—" the clerk began, but Tom Beavers interrupted him.

"I was asking because I was curious," he said. He had been studying her from the corner of his eye. Her face was beginning to show the wear of her mother's long illness, but that couldn't be called change. Changing was something she didn't seem to have done, her own style being the only one natural to her.

"I was asking," he went on, "because I saw him." He turned away from her somewhat too direct gaze and said to Totsie Poteet, whose mouth had fallen open, "It was where the new road runs close to the old road, and as far as I could tell he was right on the part of the old road where people always used to see him."

"But when?" Frances Harvey demanded.

"Last night," he told her. "Just around first dark. Driving home."

A wealth of quick feeling came up in her face. "So did I! Driving home from Jackson! I saw him, too!"

For some people, a liking for the same phonograph record or for Mayan archeology is enough of an excuse to get together. Possibly, seeing the same ghost was no more than that. Anyway, a week later, on Saturday at first dark, Frances Harvey and Tom Beavers were sitting together in a car parked just off the highway, near the spot where they agreed the ghost had appeared. The season was that long, peculiar one between summer and fall, and there were so many crickets and tree frogs going full tilt in their periphery that their voices could hardly be distinguished from the background noises, though they both would have heard a single footfall in the grass. An edge of autumn was in the air at night, and Frances had put on a tweed jacket at the last minute, so the smell of mothballs was in the car, brisk and most unghostlike.

But Tom Beavers was not going to forget the value of the ghost, whether it put in an appearance or not. His questions led Frances into reminiscence.

"No, I never saw him before the other night," she admitted. "The Negroes used to talk in the kitchen, and Regina and I—you know my sister Regina—would sit there listening, scared to go and scared to stay. Then fi-

nally going to bed upstairs was no relief, either, because
sometimes Aunt Henrietta was visiting us, and *she'd* seen
it. Or if she wasn't visiting us, the front room next to us,
where she stayed, would be empty, which was worse.
There was no way to lock ourselves in, and besides, what
was there to lock out? We'd lie all night like two sticks in
bed, and shiver. Papa finally had to take a hand. He called
us in and sat us down and said that the whole thing was
easy to explain—it was all automobiles. What their headlights did with the dust and shadows out on the Jackson
road. 'Oh, but Sammie and Jerry!' we said, with great big
eyes, sitting side by side on the sofa, with our tennis shoes
flat on the floor."

"Who were Sammie and Jerry?" asked Tom Beavers.

"Sammie was our cook. Jerry was her son, or husband,
or something. Anyway, they certainly didn't have cars.
Papa called them in. They were standing side by side by
the bookcase, and Regina and I were on the sofa—four
pairs of big eyes, and Papa pointing his finger. Papa said,
'Now, you made up these stories about ghosts, didn't
you?' 'Yes, sir,' said Sammie. 'We made them up.' 'Yes,
sir,' said Jerry. 'We sho did.' 'Well, then, you can just
stop it,' Papa said. 'See how peaked these children look?'
Sammie and Jerry were terribly polite to us for a week,
and we got in the car and rode up and down the Jackson
road at first dark to see if the headlights really did it. But
we never saw anything. We didn't tell Papa, but headlights had nothing whatever to do with it."

"You had your own *car* then?" He couldn't believe
it.

"Oh, no!" She was emphatic. "We were too young for

that. Too young to drive, really, but we did anyway."

She leaned over to let him give her cigarette a light, and saw his hand tremble. Was he afraid of the ghost or of her? She would have to stay away from talking family.

Frances remembered Tommy Beavers from her childhood—a small boy going home from school down a muddy side road alone, walking right down the middle of the road. His old aunt's house was at the bottom of a hill. It was damp there, and the yard was always muddy, with big fat chicken tracks all over it, like Egyptian writing. How did Frances know? She could not remember going there, ever. Miss Rita Beavers was said to order cold ham, mustard, bread, and condensed milk from the grocery store. "I doubt if that child ever has anything hot," Frances's mother had said once. He was always neatly dressed in the same knee pants, high socks, and checked shirt, and sat several rows ahead of Frances in study hall, right in the middle of his seat. He was three grades behind her; in those days, that much younger seemed very young indeed. What had happened to his parents? There was some story, but it was not terribly interesting, and, his people being of no importance, she had forgotten.

"I think it's past time for our ghost," she said. "He's never out so late at night."

"He gets hungry, like me," said Tom Beavers. "Are you hungry, Frances?"

They agreed on a highway restaurant where an orchestra played on weekends. Everyone went there now.

From the moment they drew up on the gravelled entrance, cheerful lights and a blare of music chased the spooks from their heads. Tom Beavers ordered well and

danced well, as it turned out. Wasn't there something she
had heard about his being "smart"? By "smart," Southern-
ers mean intellectual, and they say it in an almost conde-
scending way, smart being what you are when you can't
be anything else, and it is better, at least, than being nothing. Frances Harvey had been away enough not to look at
things from a completely Southern point of view, and she
was encouraged to discover that she and Tom had other
things in common besides a ghost, though all stemming,
perhaps, from the imagination it took to see one.

They agreed about books and favorite movies and longing to see more plays. She sighed that life in Richton was
so confining, but he assured her that Jackson could be just
as bad; *it* was getting to be like any Middle Western city,
he said, while Richton at least had a sense of the past. This
was the main reason, he went on, gaining confidence in the
jumble of commonplace noises—dishes, music, and a couple of drinkers chattering behind them—that he had
started coming back to Richton so often. He wanted to
keep a connection with the past. He lived in a modern
apartment, worked in a soundproof office—he could be in
any city. But Richton was where he had been born and
raised, and nothing could be more old-fashioned. Too
many people seemed to have their lives cut in two. He was
earnest in desiring that this should not happen to him.

"You'd better be careful," Frances said lightly. Her
mood did not incline her to profound conversation.
"There's more than one ghost in Richton. You may turn
into one yourself, like the rest of us."

"It's the last thing I'd think of you," he was quick to as-
sure her.

Had Tommy Beavers really said such a thing, in such a natural, charming way? Was Frances Harvey really so pleased? Not only was she pleased but, feeling warmly alive amid the music and small lights, she agreed with him. She would not have agreed with him more.

"I hear that Thomas Beavers has gotten to be a very attractive man," Frances Harvey's mother said unexpectedly one afternoon.

Frances had been reading aloud—Jane Austen this time. Theirs was one house where the leather-bound sets were actually read. In Jane Austen, men and women seesawed back and forth for two or three hundred pages until they struck a point of balance; then they got married. She had just put aside the book, at the end of a chapter, and risen to lower the shade against the slant of afternoon sun. "Or so Cud'n Jennie and Mrs. Giles Antley and Miss Fannie Stapleton have been coming and telling you," she said.

"People talk, of course, but the consensus is favorable," Mrs. Harvey said. "Wonders never cease; his mother ran away with a brush salesman. But nobody can make out what he's up to, coming back to Richton."

"Does he have to be 'up to' anything?" Frances asked.

"Men are always up to something," said the old lady at once. She added, more slowly, "In Thomas's case, maybe it isn't anything it oughtn't to be. They say he reads a lot. He may just have taken up with some sort of idea."

Frances stole a long glance at her mother's face on the pillow. Age and illness had reduced the image of Mrs. Harvey to a kind of caricature, centered on a mouth that Frances could not help comparing to that of a fish. There was a tension around its rim, as though it were outlined in bone, and the underlip even stuck out a little. The mouth ate, it took medicine, it asked for things, it gasped when breath was short, it commented. But when it commented, it ceased to be just a mouth and became part of Mrs. Harvey, that witty tyrant with the infallible memory for the right detail, who was at her terrible best about men.

"And what could he be thinking of?" she was wont to inquire when some man had acted foolishly. No one could ever defend accurately the man in question, and the only conclusion was Mrs. Harvey's; namely, that he wasn't thinking, if, indeed, he could. Although she had never been a belle, never a flirt, her popularity with men was always formidable. She would be observed talking marathons with one in a corner, and could you ever be sure, when they both burst into laughter, that they had not just exchanged the most shocking stories? "Of course, *he*—" she would begin later, back with the family, and the masculinity that had just been encouraged to strut and preen a little was quickly shown up as idiotic. Perhaps Mrs. Harvey hoped by this method to train her daughters away from a lot of sentimental nonsense that was their birthright as pretty Southern girls in a house with a lawn that moonlight fell on and that was often lit also by Japanese lanterns hung for parties. "Oh, he's not like that, Mama!" the little girls would cry. They were already alert for heroes who would ride up and cart them off. "Well, then, you watch," she would say. Sure enough, if you watched, she would be right.

Mrs. Harvey's younger daughter, Regina, was a credit to her mother's long campaign; she married well. The old lady, however, never tired of pointing out behind her son-in-law's back that his fondness for money was ill-concealed, that he had the longest feet she'd ever seen, and that he sometimes made grammatical errors.

Her elder daughter, Frances, on a trip to Europe, fell in love, alas! The gentleman was of French extraction but Swiss citizenship, and Frances did not marry him, because he was already married—that much filtered back to Richton. In response to a cable, she had returned home one hot July in time to witness her father's wasted face and last weeks of life. That same September, the war began. When peace came, Richton wanted to know if Frances Harvey would go back to Europe. Certain subtly complicated European matters, little understood in Richton, seemed to be obstructing Romance; one of them was probably named Money. Meanwhile, Frances's mother took to bed, in what was generally known to be her last illness.

So no one crossed the ocean, but eventually Tom Beavers came up to Mrs. Harvey's room one afternoon, to tea.

Though almost all her other faculties were seriously impaired, in ear and tongue Mrs. Harvey was as sound as a young beagle, and she could still weave a more interesting conversation than most people who go about every day and look at the world. She was of the old school of Southern lady talkers; she vexed you with no ideas, she tried to protect you from even a moment of silence. In the old days, when a bright company filled the downstairs rooms, she could keep the ball rolling amongst a crowd. Everyone—all the men especially—got their word in, but the flow of things came back to her. If one of those twenty-minutes-to-or-after silences fell—and even with her they did occur—people would turn and look at her daughter Frances. "And what do you think?" some kind-eyed gentleman would ask. Frances did not credit that she had the sort of face people would turn to, and so did not know how to take advantage of it. What did she think? Well, to answer that honestly took a moment of reflection—a fatal moment, it always turned out. Her mother would be up instructing the maid, offering someone an ashtray or another goody, or remarking outright, "Frances is so timid. She never says a word."

Tom Beavers stayed not only past teatime that day but for a drink as well. Mrs. Harvey was induced to take a glass of sherry, and now her bed became her enormous throne. Her keenest suffering as an invalid was occasioned by the absence of men. "What is a house without a man in it?" she would often cry. From her eagerness to be charming to Frances's guest that afternoon, it seemed that she would have married Tom Beavers herself if he had asked her. The amber liquid set in her small four-sided glass glowed like a jewel, and her diamond flashed; she had put on her best ring for the company. What a pity no longer to show her ankle, that delicious bone, so remarkably slender for so ample a frame.

Since the time had flown so, they all agreed enthusiastically that Tom should wait downstairs while Frances got ready to go out to dinner with him. He was hardly past the stair landing before the old lady was seized by such a fit of coughing that she could hardly speak. "It's been— It's been too much—too *much* for me!" she gasped out.

But after Frances had found the proper sedative for her, she was calmed, and insisted on having her say.

"Thomas Beavers has a good job with an insurance company in Jackson," she informed her daughter, as though Frances were incapable of finding out anything for herself. "He makes a good appearance. He is the kind of man"—she paused—"who would value a wife of good family." She stopped, panting for breath. It was this complimenting a man behind his back that was too much for her—as much out of character, and hence as much of a strain, as if she had got out of bed and tried to tap-dance.

"Heavens, Mama," Frances said, and almost giggled.

At this, the old lady, thinking the girl had made light of her suitor, half screamed at her, "Don't be so critical, Frances! You can't be so critical of men!" and fell into an even more terrible spasm of coughing. Frances had to lift her from the pillow and hold her straight until the fit passed and her breath returned. Then Mrs. Harvey's old, dry, crooked, ineradicably feminine hand was laid on her daughter's arm, and when she spoke again she shook the arm to emphasize her words.

"When your father knew he didn't have long to live," she whispered, "we discussed whether to send for you or not. You know you were his favorite, Frances. 'Suppose our girl is happy over there,' he said. 'I wouldn't want to bring her back on my account.' I said you had to have the right to choose whether to come back or not. You'd never forgive us, I said, if you didn't have the right to choose."

Frances could visualize this very conversation taking

place between her parents; she could see them, decorous
and serious, talking over the fact of his approaching death
as though it were a piece of property for agreeable disposi-
tion in the family. She could never remember him without
thinking, with a smile, how he used to come home on Sunday from church (he being the only one of them who
went) and how, immediately after hanging his hat and
cane in the hall, he would say, "Let all things proceed in
orderly progression to their final confusion. How long before dinner?" No, she had had to come home. Some
humor had always existed between them—her father and
her—and humor, of all things, cannot be betrayed.

"I meant to go back," said Frances now. "But there was
the war. At first I kept waiting for it to be over. I still
wake up at night sometimes thinking, I wonder how
much longer before the war will be over. And then—"
She stopped short. For the fact was that her lover had
been married to somebody else, and her mother was the
very person capable of pointing that out to her. Even in
the old lady's present silence she heard the unspoken
thought, and got up nervously from the bed, loosing herself from the hand on her arm, smoothing her reddish hair
where it was inclined to straggle. "And then he wrote me
that he had gone back to his wife. Her family and his had
always been close, and the war brought them back together. This was in Switzerland—naturally, he couldn't
stay on in Paris during the war. There were the children,
too—all of them were Catholic. Oh, I do understand how
it happened."

Mrs. Harvey turned her head impatiently on the pillow.
She dabbed at her moist upper lip with a crumpled linen

handkerchief; her diamond flashed once in motion. "War, religion, wife, children—yes. But men do what they want to."

Could anyone make Frances as angry as her mother could? "Believe what you like, then! You always know so much better than I do. *You* would have managed things somehow. Oh, you would have had your way!"

"Frances," said Mrs. Harvey, "I'm an old woman." The hand holding the handkerchief fell wearily, and her eyelids dropped shut. "If you should want to marry Thomas Beavers and bring him here, I will accept it. There will be no distinctions. Next, I suppose, we will be having his old deaf aunt for tea. I hope she has a hearing aid. I haven't got the strength to holler at her."

"I don't think any of these plans are necessary, Mama."

The eyelids slowly lifted. "None?"

"None."

Mrs. Harvey's breathing was as audible as a voice. She spoke, at last, without scorn, honestly. "I cannot bear the thought of leaving you alone. You, nor the house, nor your place in it—alone. I foresaw Tom Beavers here! What has he got that's better than you and this place? I knew he would come!"

Terrible as her mother's meanness was, it was not half so terrible as her love. Answering nothing, explaining nothing, Frances stood without giving in. She trembled, and tears ran down her cheeks. The two women looked at each other helplessly across the darkening room.

In the car, later that night, Tom Beavers asked, "Is your mother trying to get rid of me?" They had passed an unsatisfactory evening, and he was not going away without knowing why.

"No, it's just the other way around," said Frances, in her candid way. "She wants you so much she'd like to eat you up. She wants you in the house. Couldn't you tell?"

"She once chased me out of the yard," he recalled.

"Not really!"

They turned into Harvey Street (that was actually the name of it), and when he had drawn the car up before the dark front steps, he related the incident. He told her that Mrs. Harvey had been standing just there in the yard, talking to some visitor who was leaving by inches, the way ladies used to—ten minutes' more talk for every forward step. He, a boy not more than nine, had been crossing a corner of the lawn where a faint path had already been worn; he had had nothing to do with wearing the path, and had taken it quite innocently and openly. "You, boy!" Mrs. Harvey's fan was an enormous painted thing. She had furled it with a clack so loud he could still hear it. "You don't cut through my yard again! Now, you stop where you are and you go all the way back around by the walk, and don't you ever ever do that again." He went back and all the way around. She was fanning comfortably as he passed. "Old Miss Rita Beavers' nephew," he heard her say, and though he did not speak of it now to Frances, Mrs. Harvey's rich tone had been as stuffed with wickedness as a fruitcake with goodies. In it you could have found so many things: that, of course, he didn't know any better, that he was poor, that she knew his first name but would not deign to mention it, that she meant him to understand all this and more. Her fan was probably still somewhere in the house, he reflected. If he ever opened the wrong door, it might fall from above and brain him. It seemed impossible that nowadays he could even have the chance to open the wrong door in the Harvey house. With its graceful rooms and big lawn, its camellias and magnolia trees, the house had been one of the enchanted castles of his childhood, and Frances and Regina Harvey had been two princesses running about the lawn one Saturday morning drying their hair with big white towels and not noticing when he passed.

There was a strong wind that evening. On the way home, Frances and Tom had noticed how the night was streaming, but whether with mist or dust or the smoke from some far-off fire in the dry winter woods they could not tell. As they stood on the sidewalk, the clouds raced over them, and moonlight now and again came through. A limb rubbed against a high cornice. Inside the screened area of the porch, the swing jangled its iron chains. Frances's coat blew about her, and her hair blew. She felt herself to be no different from anything there that the wind was blowing on, her happiness of no relevance in the dark torrent of nature.

"I can't leave her, Tom. But I can't ask you to live with her, either. Of all the horrible ideas! She'd make demands, take all my time, laugh at you behind your back—she has to run everything. You'd hate me in a week."

He did not try to pretty up the picture, because he had a feeling that it was all too accurate. Now, obviously, was the time she should go on to say there was no good his waiting around through the years for her. But hearts are not noted for practicality, and Frances stood with her hair blowing, her hands stuck in her coat pockets, and did not go on to say anything. Tom pulled her close to him—in, as it were, out of the wind.

"I'll be coming by next weekend, just like I've been doing. And the next one, too," he said. "We'll just leave it that way, if it's O.K. with you."

"Oh, yes, it is, Tom!" Never so satisfied to be weak, she kissed him and ran inside.

He stood watching on the walk until her light flashed on. Well, he had got what he was looking for; a connection with the past, he had said. It was right upstairs, a splendid old mass of dictatorial female flesh, thinking about him. Well, they could go on, he and Frances, sitting on either side of a sickbed, drinking tea and sipping sherry, with streaks of gray broadening on their brows, while the familiar seasons came and went. So he thought. Like Frances, he believed that the old lady had a stranglehold on life.

Suddenly, in March, Mrs. Harvey died.

A heavy spring funeral, with lots of roses and other scented flowers in the house, is the worst kind of all. There is something so recklessly fecund about a South Mississippi spring that death becomes just another word in the dictionary, along with swarms of others, and even so pure and white a thing as a gardenia has too heavy a scent and may suggest decay. Mrs. Harvey, amid such odors, sank to rest with a determined pomp, surrounded by admiring eyes.

While Tom Beavers did not "sit with the family" at this time, he was often observed with the Harveys, and there was whispered speculation among those who were at the church and the cemetery that the Harvey house might soon come into new hands, "after a decent interval." No one would undertake to judge for a Harvey how long an interval was decent.

Frances suffered from insomnia in the weeks that followed, and at night she wandered about the spring-swollen air of the old house, smelling now spring and now death. "Let all things proceed in orderly progression to their final confusion." She had always thought that the final confusion referred to death, but now she began to think that it could happen any time; that final confusion, having found the door ajar, could come into a house and show no inclination to leave. The worrisome thing, the thing it all came back to, was her mother's clothes. They were numerous, expensive, and famous, and Mrs. Harvey had never discarded any of them. If you opened a closet door, hatboxes as big as crates towered above your head. The shiny black trim of a great shawl stuck out of a wardrobe door just below the lock. Beneath the lid of a cedar chest, the bright eyes of a tippet were ready to twinkle at you. And the jewels! Frances's sister had restrained her from burying them all on their mother, and had even gone off with a wad of them tangled up like fishing tackle in an envelope, on the ground of promises made now and again in the course of the years.

("Regina," said Frances, "what else were you two talking about besides jewelry?" "I don't remember," said Regina, getting mad.

"Frances makes me so mad," said Regina to her husband as they were driving home. "I guess I can love Mama and jewelry, too. Mama certainly loved *us* and jewelry, too.")

One afternoon, Frances went out to the cemetery to take two wreaths sent by somebody who had "just heard." She drove out along the winding cemetery road, stopping the car a good distance before she reached the gate, in order to walk through the woods. The dogwood was beautiful that year. She saw a field where a house used to stand but had burned down; its cedar trees remained, and two bushes of bridal wreath marked where the front gate had swung. She stopped to admire the clusters of white bloom massing up through the young, feathery leaf and stronger now than the leaf itself. In the woods, the redbud was a smoke along shadowy ridges, and the dogwood drifted in layers, like snow suspended to give you all the time you needed to wonder at it. But why, she wondered, do they call it bridal *wreath?* It's not a wreath but a little bouquet. Wreaths are for funerals, anyway. As if to prove it, she looked down at the two she held, one in each hand. She walked on, and such complete desolation came over her that it was more of a wonder than anything in the woods—more, even, than death.

As she returned to the car from the two parallel graves, she met a thin, elderly, very light-skinned Negro man in the road. He inquired if she would mind moving her car so that he could pass. He said that there was a sick colored girl in his wagon, whom he was driving in to the doctor. He pointed out politely that she had left her car right in the middle of the road. "Oh, I'm terribly sorry," said Frances, and hurried off toward the car.

That night, reading late in bed, she thought, I could

have given her a ride into town. No wonder they talk
about us up North. A mile into town in a wagon! She
might have been having a baby. She became conscience-
stricken about it—foolishly so, she realized, but if you
start worrying about something in a house like the one
Frances Harvey lived in, in the dead of night, alone, you
will go on worrying about it until dawn. She was out of
sleeping pills.

She remembered having bought a fresh box of sedatives
for her mother the day before she died. She got up and
went into her mother's closed room, where the bed had
been dismantled for airing, its wooden parts propped along
the walls. On the closet shelf she found the shoe box into
which she had packed away the familiar articles of the
bedside table. Inside she found the small enamelled-card-
board box, with the date and prescription inked on the
cover in Totsie Poteet's somewhat prissy handwriting, but
the box was empty. She was surprised, for she realized that
her mother could have used only one or two of the pills.
Frances was so determined to get some sleep that she
searched the entire little store of things in the shoe box
quite heartlessly, but there were no pills. She returned to
her room and tried to read, but could not, and so smoked
instead and stared out at the dawn-blackening sky. The
house sighed. She could not take her mind off the Negro
girl. If she died . . . When it was light, she dressed and
got into the car.

In town, the postman was unlocking the post office to
sort the early mail. "I declare," he said to the rural mail
carrier who arrived a few minutes later, "Miss Frances
Harvey is driving herself crazy. Going back out yonder to

the cemetery, and it not seven o'clock in the morning."

"Aw," said the rural deliveryman skeptically, looking at the empty road.

"That's right. I was here and seen her. You wait there, you'll see her come back. She'll drive herself nuts. Them old maids like that, left in them old houses—crazy and sweet, or crazy and mean, or just plain crazy. They just ain't locked up like them that's down in the asylum. That's the only difference."

"Miss Frances Harvey ain't no more than thirty-two, -three years old."

"Then she's just got more time to get crazier in. You'll see."

That day was Friday, and Tom Beavers, back from Jackson, came up Frances Harvey's sidewalk, as usual, at exactly a quarter past seven in the evening. Frances was not "going out" yet, and Regina had telephoned her long distance to say that "in all probability" she should not be receiving gentlemen "in." "What would Mama say?" Regina asked. Frances said she didn't know, which was not true, and went right on cooking dinners for Tom every weekend.

In the dining room that night, she sat across one corner of the long table from Tom. The useless length of polished cherry stretched away from them into the shadows as sadly as a road. Her plate pushed back, her chin resting on one palm, Frances stirred her coffee and said, "I don't know what on earth to do with all of Mama's clothes. I can't give them away, I can't sell them, I can't burn them, and the attic is full already. What can I do?"

"You look better tonight," said Tom.

"I slept," said Frances. "I slept and slept. From early this morning until just 'while ago. I never slept so well."

Then she told him about the Negro near the cemetery the previous afternoon, and how she had driven back out there as soon as dawn came, and found him again. He had been walking across the open field near the remains of the house that had burned down. There was no path to him from her, and she had hurried across ground uneven from old plowing and covered with the kind of small, tender grass it takes a very skillful mule to crop. "Wait!" she had cried. "Please wait!" The Negro had stopped and waited for her to reach him. "Your daughter?" she asked, out of breath.

"Daughter?" he repeated.

"The colored girl that was in the wagon yesterday. She was sick, you said, so I wondered. I could have taken her to town in the car, but I just didn't think. I wanted to know, how is she? Is she very sick?"

He had removed his old felt nigger hat as she approached him. "She a whole lot better, Miss Frances. She going to be all right now." Then he smiled at her. He did not say thank you, or anything more. Frances turned and walked back to the road and the car. And exactly as though the recovery of the Negro girl in the wagon had been her own recovery, she felt the return of a quiet breath and a steady pulse, and sensed the blessed stirring of a morning breeze. Up in her room, she had barely time to draw an old quilt over her before she fell asleep.

"When I woke, I knew about Mama," she said now to Tom. By the deepened intensity of her voice and eyes, it was plain that this was the important part. "It isn't right to say I *knew*," she went on, "because I had known all the time—ever since last night. I just realized it, that's all. I realized she had killed herself. It had to be that."

He listened soberly through the story about the box of sedatives. "But why?" he asked her. "It maybe looks that way, but what would be her reason for doing it?"

"Well, you see—" Frances said, and stopped.

Tom Beavers talked quietly on. "She didn't suffer. With what she had, she could have lived five, ten, who knows how many years. She was well cared for. Not hard up, I wouldn't say. Why?"

The pressure of his questioning could be insistent, and her trust in him, even if he was nobody but old Miss Rita Beavers' nephew, was well-nigh complete. "Because of you and me," she said, finally. "I'm certain of it, Tom. She didn't want to stand in our way. She never knew how to express love, you see." Frances controlled herself with an effort.

He did not reply, but sat industriously balancing a match folder on the tines of an unused serving fork. Anyone who has passed a lonely childhood in the company of an old deaf aunt is not inclined to doubt things hastily, and Tom Beavers would not have said he disbelieved anything Frances had told him. In fact, it seemed only too real to him. Almost before his eyes, that imperial, practical old hand went fumbling for the pills in the dark. But there had been much more to it than just love, he reflected. Bitterness, too, and pride, and control. And humor, perhaps, and the memory of a frightened little boy chased out of the yard by a twitch of her fan. Being invited to tea was one thing; suicide was quite another. Times had certainly changed, he thought.

But, of course, he could not say that he believed it, either. There was only Frances to go by. The match folder came to balance and rested on the tines. He glanced up at her, and a chill walked up his spine, for she was too serene. Cheek on palm, a lock of reddish hair fallen forward, she was staring at nothing with the absorbed silence of a child, or of a sweet, silver-haired old lady engaged in memory. Soon he might find that more and more of her was vanishing beneath this placid surface.

He himself did not know what he had seen that Friday evening so many months ago—what the figure had been that stood forward from the roadside at the tilt of the curve and urgently waved an arm to him. By the time he had braked and backed, the man had disappeared. Maybe it had been somebody drunk (for Richton had plenty of those to offer), walking it off in the cool of the woods at first dark. No such doubts had occurred to Frances. And what if he told her now the story Totsie had related of the road gang and the sick Negro girl in the wagon? Another labyrinth would open before her; she would never get out.

In Richton, the door to the past was always wide open, and what came in through it and went out of it had made people "different." But it scarcely ever happens, even in Richton, that one is able to see the precise moment when fact becomes faith, when life turns into legend, and people start to bend their finest loyalties to make themselves bemused custodians of the grave. Tom Beavers saw that moment now, in the profile of this dreaming girl, and he knew there was no time to lose.

He dropped the match folder into his coat pocket. "I think we should be leaving, Frances."

"Oh, well, I don't know about going out yet," she said. "People criticize you so. Regina even had the nerve to telephone. Word had got all the way to her that you came here to have supper with me and we were alone in the house. When I tell the maid I want biscuits made up for two people, she looks like 'What would yo mama say?' "

"I mean," he said, "I think it's time we left for good."

"And never came back?" It was exactly like Frances to balk at going to a movie but seriously consider an elopement.

"Well, never is a long time. I like to see about Aunt Rita every once in a great while. She can't remember from one time to the next whether it's two days or two years since I last came."

She glanced about the walls and at the furniture, the pictures, and the silver. "But I thought you would want to live here, Tom. It never occurred to me. I know it never occurred to Mama . . . This house . . . It can't be just left."

"It's a fine old house," he agreed. "But what would we do with all your mother's clothes?"

Her freckled hand remained beside the porcelain cup for what seemed a long time. He waited and made no move toward her; he felt her uncertainty keenly, but he believed that some people should not be startled out of a spell.

"It's just as you said," he went on, finally. "You can't give them away, you can't sell them, you can't burn them, and you can't put them in the attic, because the attic is full already. So what are you going to do?"

Between them, the single candle flame achieved a silent altitude. Then, politely, as on any other night, though shaking back her hair in a decided way, she said, "Just let me get my coat, Tom."

She locked the door when they left, and put the key under the mat—a last obsequy to the house. Their hearts were bounding ahead faster than they could walk down the sidewalk or drive off in the car, and, mindful, perhaps, of what happened to people who did, they did not look back.

Had they done so, they would have seen that the Harvey house was more beautiful than ever. All unconscious of its rejection by so mere a person as Tom Beavers, it seemed, instead, to have got rid of what did not suit it, to be free, at last, to enter with abandon the land of mourning and shadows and memory.

Ship Island

The Story of a Mermaid

The French book was lying open on a corner of the dining-room table, between the floor lamp and the window. The floor lamp, which had come with the house, had a cover made of green glass, with a fringe. The French book must have lain just that way for two months. Nancy, coming in from the beach, tried not to look at it. It reminded her of how much she had meant to accomplish during the summer, of the strong sense of intent, something like refinement, with which she had chosen just that spot for studying. It was out of hearing of the conversations with the neighbors that went on every evening out on the side porch, it had window light in the daytime and lamplight at night, it had a small, slanting view of the beach, and it drew a breeze. The pencils were still there, still sharp, and the exercise, broken off. She sometimes stopped to read it over. "The soldiers of the emperor were crossing the bridge: *Les soldats de l'empereur traversaient le pont.* The officer has already knocked at the gate: *L'officier a déjà frappé*—" She could not have finished that sentence now if she had sat right down and tried.

Nancy could no longer find herself in relation to the girl who had sought out such a good place to study, had sharpened the pencils and opened the book and sat down to bend over it. What she did know was how—just now, when she had been down at the beach, across the boulevard—the sand scuffed beneath her step and shells lay strewn about, chipped and disorderly, near the water's edge. Some shells were empty; some, with damp drying down their backs, went for short walks. Far out, a long white shelf of cloud indicated a distance no gull could dream of gaining, though the gulls spun tirelessly up, dazzling in the white light that comes just as morning vanishes. A troop of pelicans sat like curiously carved knobs on the tops of a long series of wooden piles, which were spaced out at intervals in the water. The piles were what was left of a private pier blown away by a hurricane some years ago.

Nancy had been alone on the beach. Behind her, the boulevard glittered in the morning sun and the season's traffic rocked by the long curve of the shore in the clumps of breasting speed. She stood looking outward at the high straight distant shelf of cloud. The islands were out there, plainly visible. The walls of the old Civil War fort on the nearest one of them, the one with the lighthouse—Ship Island—were plain today as well. She had been out there once this summer with Rob Acklen, out there on the island, where the reeds grew in the wild white sand, and the water teemed so thick with seaweed that only crazy people would have tried to swim in it. The gulf had rushed white and strong through all the seaweed, frothing up the beach. On the beach, the froth turned brown, the color of softly moving crawfish claws. In the boat coming home through the sunset that day, a boy standing up in the pilothouse played "Over the Waves" on his harmonica. Rob Acklen had put his jacket around Nancy's shoulders—she had never thought to bring a sweater. The jacket swallowed her; it smelled more like Rob than he did. The boat moved, the breeze blew, the sea swelled, all to the lilt of the music. All twenty-five members of the Laurel, Mississippi, First Baptist Church Adult Bible Class, who had come out with them on the excursion boat, and to whom Rob and Nancy had yet to introduce themselves, had stopped giggling and making their silly jokes. They were tired, and stood in a huddle like sheep; they were shaped like sheep as well, with little shoulders and wide bottoms—it was somehow sad. Nancy and Rob, young and trim, stood side by side near the bow, like figureheads of the boat, hearing the music and watching the thick prow butt the swell, which the sunset had stained a deep red. Nancy felt for certain that this was the happiest she had ever been.

Alone on the sand this morning, she had spread out her beach towel and stood for a moment looking up the beach, way up, past a grove of live oaks to where Rob Acklen's house was visible. He would be standing in the kitchen, in loafers and a dirty white shirt and an old pair of shorts, drinking cold beer from the refrigerator right out of the can. He would eat lunch with his mother and sister, read the paper and write a letter, then dress and drive into town to help his father in the office, going right past Nancy's house along the boulevard. Around three, he would call her up. He did this every day. His name was Fitzrobert Conroy Acklen—one of those full-blown Con-

federate names. Everybody liked him, and more than a
few—a general mixture of every color, size, age, sex, and
religion—would say when he passed by, "I declare, I just
love that boy." So he was bound to have a lot of nick-
names: "Fitz" or "Bobbie" or "Cousin" or "Son"—he answered to almost anything. He was the kind of boy people
have high, undefined hopes for. He had first seen Nancy
Lewis one morning when he came by her house to make
an insurance call for his father.

Breaking off her French—could it have been the sentence about *"l'officier"*?—she had gone out to see who it
was. She was expecting Mrs. Nattier, their neighbor, who
had skinny white freckled legs she never shaved and
whose husband, "off" somewhere, was thought not to be
doing well; or Mrs. Nattier's little boy Bernard, who
thought it was fun to hide around corners after dark and
jump out saying nothing more original than "Boo!"
(Once, he had screamed "Raw head and bloody bones!,"
but Nancy was sure somebody had told him to); or one of
the neighbor ladies in the back—old Mrs. Poultney, whom
they rented from and who walked with a cane, or Miss
Henriette Dupré, who was so devout she didn't even have
to go to confession before weekday Communion and
whose hands, always tucked up in the sleeves of her sack,
were as cold as church candles, and to think of them
touching you was like rabbits skipping over your grave on
dark rainy nights in winter up in the lonely wet-leaf-
covered hills. Or else it was somebody wanting to be paid
something. Nancy had opened the door and looked up,
and there, instead of a dozen other people, was Rob Acklen.

Not that she knew his name. She had seen boys like him

down on the coast, ever since her family had moved there from Little Rock back in the spring. She had seen them playing tennis on the courts back of the hotel, where she sometimes went to jump on the trampoline. She believed that the hotel people thought she was on the staff in some sort of way, as she was about the right age for that—just a year or so beyond high school but hardly old enough to work in town. The weather was already getting hot, and the season was falling off. When she passed the courts, going and coming, she saw the boys out of the corner of her eye. Were they really so much taller than the boys up where they had moved from, up in Arkansas? They were lankier and a lot more casual. They were more assured. To Nancy, whose family was in debt and whose father, in one job after another, was always doing something wrong, the boys playing tennis had that wonderful remoteness of creatures to be admired on the screen, or those seen in whiskey ads, standing near the bar of a country club and sleekly talking about things she could not begin to imagine. But now here was one, in a heavy tan cotton suit and a light blue shirt with a buttoned-down collar and dark tie, standing on her own front porch and smiling at her.

Yet when Rob called Nancy for a date, a day or two later, she didn't have to be told that he did it partly because he liked to do nice things for people. He obviously liked to be considerate and kind, because the first time he saw her he said, "I guess you don't know many people yet?"

"No, because Daddy just got transferred," she said—"transferred" being her mother's word for it; fired was what it was. She gave him a Coke and talked to him awhile, standing around in the house, which unaccountably continued to be empty. She said she didn't know a thing about insurance.

Now, still on the beach, Nancy Lewis sat down in the middle of her beach towel and began to rub suntan lotion on her neck and shoulders. Looking down the other way, away from Rob's house and toward the yacht club, she saw a man standing alone on the sand. She had not noticed him before. He was facing out toward the gulf and staring fixedly at the horizon. He was wearing shorts and a shirt made out of red bandanna, with the tail out—a stout young man with black hair.

Just then, without warning, it began to rain. There were no clouds one could see in the overhead dazzle, but it rained anyway; the drops fell in huge discs, marking the sand, and splashing on Nancy's skin. Each drop seemed enough to fill a Dixie cup. At first, Nancy did not know what the stinging sensation was; then she knew the rain was burning her. It was scalding hot! Strange, outlandish, but also painful, was how she found it. She jumped up and began to flinch and twist away, trying to escape, and a moment later she had snatched up her beach towel and flung it around her shoulders. But the large hot drops kept falling, and there was no escape from them. She started rubbing her cheek and forehead and felt that she might blister all over; then, since it kept on and on and was all so inexplicable, she grabbed her lotion and ran up the beach and out of the sand and back across the boulevard. Once in her own front yard, under the scraggy trees, she felt the rain no longer, and looked back curiously into the dazzle beyond the boulevard.

"I thought you meant to stay for a while," her mother

said. "Was it too hot? Anybody would be crazy to go out there now. There's never anybody out there at this time of day."

"It was all right," said Nancy, "but it started raining. I never felt anything like it. The rain was so hot it burned me. Look. My face—" She ran to look in the mirror. Sure enough, her face and shoulders looked splotched. It might blister. I might be scarred for life, she thought—one of those dramatic phrases left over from high school.

Nancy's mother, Mrs. Lewis, was a discouraged lady whose silky, blondish-grey hair was always slipping loose and tagging out around her face. She would not try to improve herself and talked a lot in company about her family; two of her uncles had been professors simultaneously at the University of North Carolina. One of them had written a book on phonetics. Mrs. Lewis seldom found anyone who had heard of them, or of the book, either. Some people asked what phonetics were, and others did not ask anything at all.

Mrs. Lewis now said to her daughter, "You just got too much sun."

"No, it was the rain. It was really scalding hot."

"I never heard of such a thing," her mother said. "Out of a clear sky."

"I can't help that," Nancy said. "I guess I ought to know."

Mrs. Lewis took on the kind of look she had when she would open the handkerchief drawer of a dresser and see two used, slightly bent carpet nails, some Scotch Tape melted together, an old receipt, an unanswered letter announcing a cousin's wedding, some scratched negatives saved for someone but never developed, some dusty foreign coins, a bank deposit book from a town they lived in during the summer before Nancy was born, and an old telegram whose contents, forgotten, no one would dare now to explore, for it would say something awful but absolutely true.

"I wish you wouldn't speak to me like that," Mrs. Lewis said. "All I know is, it certainly didn't rain here."

Nancy wandered away, into the dining room. She felt bad about everything—about quarrelling with her mother, about not getting a suntan, about wasting her time all summer with Rob Acklen and not learning any French. She went and took a long cool bath in the big old bathroom, where the bathtub had ball-and-claw feet painted mustard yellow and the single light bulb on the long cord dropped down one mile from the stratosphere.

What the Lewises found in a rented house was always outclassed by what they brought into it. Nancy's father, for instance, had a china donkey that bared its teeth in a great big grin. Written on one side was "If you really want to look like me" and on the other "Just keep right on talking." Her father loved the donkey and its message, and always put it on the living-room table of whatever house they were in. When he got a drink before dinner each evening, he would wander back with glass in hand and look the donkey over. "That's pretty good," he would say just before he took the first swallow. Nancy had often longed to break the donkey, by accident—that's what she would say, that it had all been an accident—but she couldn't get over the feeling that if she did, worse things than the Lewises had ever imagined would happen to them. That donkey would let in a flood of trouble, that she knew.

After Nancy got out of the tub and dried, she rubbed Jergens Lotion on all the splotches the rain had made. Then she ate a peanut-butter sandwich and more shrimp salad left over from supper the night before, and drank a cold Coke. Now and then, eating, she would go look in the mirror. By the time Rob Acklen called up, the red marks had all but disappeared.

That night, riding down to Biloxi with Rob, Nancy confided that the catalogue of people she disliked, headed by Bernard Nattier, included every single person—Miss Henriette Dupré, Mrs. Poultney, and Mrs. Nattier, and Mr. Nattier, too, when he was at home—that she had to be with these days. It even included, she was sad to say, her mother and father. If Bernard Nattier had to be mean—and it was clear he did have to—why did he have to be so corny? He put wads of wet, chewed bubble gum in her purses—that was the most original thing he ever did. Otherwise, it was just live crawfish in her bed or crabs in her shoes; anybody could think of that. And when he stole, he took things *she* wanted, nothing simple, like money—she could have forgiven him for that—but cigarettes, lipstick, and ashtrays she had stolen herself here and there. If she locked her door, he got in through the window; if she locked the window, she suffocated. Not only that, but he would crawl out from under the bed. His eyes were slightly crossed and he knew how to turn the lids back on themselves so that it looked like blood, and then he would chase her. He was browned to the color of dirt all over and he smelled like salt mud the sun had dried. He wore black tennis shoes laced too tight at the ankles and from sunup till way past dark he never thought of anything but what to do to Nancy, and she would have liked to kill him.

She made Rob Acklen laugh. She amused him. He didn't take anything Nancy Lewis could say at all to heart, but, as if she was something he had found on the beach and was teaching to talk, he, with his Phi Beta Kappa key and his good level head and his wonderful prospects, found everything she told about herself cute, funny, absurd. He did remark that he had such feelings himself from time to time—that he would occasionally get crazy mad at one of his parents or the other, and that he once planned his sister's murder down to the last razor slash. But he laughed again, and his chewing gum popped amiably in his jaws. When she told him about the hot rain, he said he didn't believe it. He said "Aw," which was what a boy like Rob Acklen said when he didn't believe something. The top of his old white Mercury convertible was down and the wind rushed past like an endless bolt of raw silk being drawn against Nancy's cheek.

In the ladies'-room mirror at the Beach View, where they stopped to eat, she saw the bright quality of her eyes, as though she had been drinking. Her skirts rustled in the narrow room; a porous white disc of deodorant hung on a hook, fuming the air. Her eyes, though blue, looked startlingly dark in her pale skin, for though she tried hard all the time, she never seemed to tan. All the sun did, as her mother was always pointing out, was bleach her hair three shades lighter; a little more and it would be almost white.

Out on the island that day, out on Ship Island, she had
drifted in the water like seaweed, with the tide combing
her limbs and hair, tugging her through lengths of fuzzy
water growth. She had lain flat on her face with her arms
stretched out before her, experiencing the curious lift the
water's motion gave to the tentacles of weed, wondering
whether she liked it or not. Did something alive clamber
the small of her back? Did something wishful grope the
spiral of her ear? Rob had caught her wrist hard and
waked her—waked was what he did, though to sleep in
water is not possible. He said he thought she had been
there too long. "Nobody can keep their face in the water
that long," was what he said.

"I did," said Nancy.

Rob's brow had been blistered a little, she recalled, for
that had been back early in the summer, soon after they
had met—but the changes the sun made on him went
without particular attention. The seasons here were old
ground to him. He said that the island was new, however—or at least forgotten. He said he had never been
there but once, and that many years ago, on a Boy Scout
picnic. Soon they were exploring the fort, reading the
dates off the metal signs whose letters glowed so smoothly
in the sun, and the brief summaries of what those little
boys, little military-academy boys turned into soldiers, had
endured. Not old enough to fill up the name of soldier, or
of prisoner, either, which is what they were—not old
enough to shave, Nancy bet—still, they had died there,
miserably far from home, and had been buried in the sand.
There was a lot more. Rob would have been glad to read
all about it, but she wasn't interested. What they knew al-

ready was plenty, just about those boys. A bright, worried
lizard ran out of a hot rubble of brick. They came out of
the fort and walked alone together eastward toward the
dunes, now skirting near the shore that faced the sound
and now wandering south, where they could hear or
sometimes glimpse the gulf. They were overlooked all the
way by an old white lighthouse. From far away behind,
the twenty-five members of the Adult Bible Class could be
overheard playing a silly, shrill Sunday-school game. It
came across the ruins of the fort and the sad story of the
dead soldiers like something that had happened long ago
that you could not quite remember having joined in. On
the beach to their right, toward the gulf, a flock of sand-
pipers with blinding-white breasts stepped pecking along
the water's edge, and on the inner beach, toward the
sound, a wrecked sailboat with a broken mast lay half
buried in the sand.

Rob kept teasing her along, pulling at the soft wool
strings of her bathing suit, which knotted at the nape and
again under her shoulder blades, worrying loose the damp
hair that she had carefully slicked back and pinned.
"There isn't anybody in that house," he assured her, some
minutes later, having explored most of that part of the island and almost as much of Nancy as well, having almost,
but not quite—his arms around her—coaxed and caressed
her down to ground level in a clump of reeds. "There
hasn't been in years and years," he said, encouraging her.

"It's only those picnic people," she said, holding off, for
the reeds would not have concealed a medium-sized
mouse. They had been to look at the sailboat and thought
about climbing inside (kissing closely, they had almost

fallen right over into it), but it did have a rotten tin can in the bottom and smelled, so here they were back out in the dunes.

"They've got to drink all those Coca-Colas," Rob said, "and give out all those prizes, and anyway—"

She never learned anyway what, but it didn't matter. Maybe she began to make up all that the poor little soldiers had missed out on. The island's very spine, a warm reach of thin ground, came smoothly up into the arch of her back; and it was at least halfway the day itself, with its fair, wide-open eyes, that she went over to. She felt somewhat historical afterward, as though they had themselves added one more mark to all those that place remembered.

Having played all the games and given out the prizes, having eaten all the homemade cookies and drunk the case of soft drinks just getting warm, and gone sightseeing through the fort, the Bible Class was now coming, too, crying "Yoohoo!," to explore the island. They discovered Rob hurling shells and bits of rock into the surf, while Nancy, scavenging a little distance away, tugged up out of the sand a shell so extraordinary it was worth showing around. It was purple, pink, and violet inside—a palace of colors; the king of the oysters had no doubt lived there. When she held it shyly out to them, they cried "Look!" and "Ooo!," so there was no need for talking to them much at all, and in the meantime the evening softened, the water glowed, the glare dissolved. Far out, there were other islands one could see now, and beyond those must be many more. They had been there all along.

Going home, Nancy gave the wonderful shell to the boy who stood in the pilothouse playing "Over the

Waves." She glanced back as they walked off up the pier
and saw him look at the shell, try it for weight, and then
throw it in the water, leaning far back on his arm and putting a good spin on the throw, the way boys like to
do—the way Rob Acklen himself had been doing, too, just
that afternoon.

"Why did you do that?" Rob had demanded. He was
frowning; he looked angry. He had thought they should
keep the shell—to remember, she supposed.

"For the music," she explained.

"But it was ours," he said. When she didn't answer, he
said again, "Why did you, Nancy?"

But still she didn't answer.

When Nancy returned to their table at the Beach View,
having put her lipstick back straight after eating fish, Rob
was paying the check. "Why not believe me?" she asked
him. "It was true. The rain was hot as fire. I thought I
would be scarred for life."

It was still broad daylight, not even twilight. In the
bright, air-conditioned restaurant, the light from the water
glazed flatly against the broad picture windows, the chan-
deliers, and the glasses. It was the hour when mirrors re-
flect nothing and bars look tired. The restaurant was a
boozy, cheap sort of place with a black-lined gambling
hall in the back, but everyone went there because the food
was good.

"You're just like Mama," she said. "You think I made it
up."

Rob said, teasing, "I didn't say that. I just said I didn't
believe it." He loved getting her caught in some sort of

logic she couldn't get out of. When he opened the door for her, she got a good sidelong view of his longish, firm face and saw the way his somewhat fine brows arched up with one or two bright reddish hairs in among the dark ones; his hair was that way, too, when the sun hit it. Maybe, if nobody had told him, he wouldn't have known it; he seemed not to notice so very much about himself. Having the confidence of people who don't worry much, his grin could snare her instantly—a glance alone could make her feel how lucky she was he'd ever noticed her. But it didn't do at all to think about him now. It would be ages before they made it through the evening and back, retracing the way and then turning off to the bayou, and even then, there would be those mosquitoes.

Bayou lovemaking suited Rob just fine; he was one of those people mosquitoes didn't bite. They certainly bit Nancy. They were huge and silent, and the minute the car stopped they would even come and sit upon her eyelids, if she closed her eyes, a dozen to each tender arc of flesh. They would gather on her face, around her nose and mouth. Clothlike, like rags and tatters, like large dry ashes of burnt cloth, they came in lazy droves, in fleets, sailing on the air. They were never in any hurry, being every-where at once and always ready to bite. Nancy had been known to jump all the way out of the car and go stamping across the grass like a calf. She grew sulky and despairing and stood on one leg at a time in the moonlight, slapping at her ankles, while Rob leaned his chin on the doorframe and watched her with his affectionate, total interest.

Nancy, riddled and stinging with beads of actual blood briar-pointed here and there upon her, longed to be almost

anywhere else—she especially longed for New Orleans.
She always talked about it, although, never having been
there, she had to say the things that other people said—food
and jazz in the French Quarter, beer and crabs out on
Lake Pontchartrain. Rob said vaguely they would go
sometime. But she could tell that things were wrong for
him at this point. "The food's just as good around here,"
he said.

"Oh, Rob!" She knew it wasn't so. She could feel that
city, hanging just over the horizon from them scarcely
fifty miles away, like some swollen bronze moon, at once
brilliant and shadowy and drenched in every sort of amplified smell. Rob was stroking her hair, and in time his repeated, gentle touch gained her attention. It seemed to tell
what he liked—girls all spanking clean, with scrubbed fin-
gernails, wearing shoes still damp with white shoe polish.
Even a fresh gardenia stuck in their hair wouldn't be too
much for him. There would be all sorts of differences, to
him, between Ship Island and the French Quarter, but she
did not have much idea just what they were. Nancy took
all this in, out of his hand on her head. She decided she
had better not talk anymore about New Orleans. She
wriggled around, looking out over his shoulder, through
the moonlight, toward where the pitch-black surface of
the bayou water showed in patches through the trees. The
trees were awful, hung with great spooky gray tatters of
Spanish moss. Nancy was reminded of the house she and
her family were living in; it had recently occurred to her
that the peculiar smell it had must come from some Spanish moss that had got sealed in behind the panelling, between the walls. The moss was alive in there and growing,

and that was where she was going to seal Bernard Nattier up someday, for him to see how it felt. She had tried to kill him once, by filling her purse with rocks and oyster shells—the roughest she could find. She had read somewhere that this weapon was effective for ladies in case of attack. But he had ducked when she swung the purse at him, and she had only gone spinning round and round, falling at last into a camellia tree, which had scratched her. . . .

"The Skeltons said for us to stop by there for a drink," Rob told her. They were driving again, and the car was back on the boulevard, in the still surprising daylight. "What did you say?" he asked her.

"Nothing."

"You just don't want to go?"

"No, I don't much want to go."

"Well, then, we won't stay long."

The Skelton house was right on the water, with a second-story, glassed-in, air-conditioned living room looking out over the sound. The sofas and chairs were covered with gold-and-white striped satin, and the room was full of Rob's friends. Lorna Skelton, who had been Rob's girl the summer before and who dressed so beautifully, was handing drinks round and saying, "So which is your favorite bayou, Rob?" She had a sort of fake "good sport" tone of voice and wanted to appear ready for anything. (Being so determined to be nice around Nancy, she was going to fall right over backward one day.)

"Do I have to have a favorite?" Rob asked. "They all look good to me. Full of slime and alligators."

"I should have asked Nancy."

"They're all full of mosquitos," Nancy said, hoping that was O.K. for an answer. She thought that virgins were awful people.

"Trapped, boy!" Turner Carmichael said to Rob, and banged him on the shoulder. Turner wanted to be a writer, so he thought it was all right to tell people about themselves. "Women will be your downfall, Acklen. Nancy, honey, you haven't spoken to the General."

Old General Skelton, Lorna's grandfather, sat in the corner of the living room near the mantel, drinking a Scotch highball. You had to shout at him.

"How's the election going, General?" Turner asked.

"Election? Election? What election? Oh, the election! Well—" He lowered his voice, confidentially. As with most deaf people, his tone went to extremes. "There's no question of it. The one we want is the one we know. Know Houghman's father. Knew his grandfather. His stand is the same, identical one that we are all accustomed to. On every subject—this race thing especially. Very dangerous now. Extremely touchy. But Houghman—absolute! Never experiment, never question, never turn back. These are perilous times."

"Yes, sir," said Turner, nodding in an earnestly false way, which was better than the earnestly impressed way a younger boy at the General's elbow shouted, "General Skelton, that's just what my daddy says!"

"Oh, yes," said the old man, sipping Scotch. "Oh, yes, it's true. And you, Missy?" he thundered suddenly at Nancy, making her jump. "Are you just visiting here?"

"Why, Granddaddy," Lorna explained, joining them, "Nancy lives here now. You know Nancy."

"Then why isn't she tan?" the old man continued. "Why so pale and wan, fair nymph?"

"Were you a nymph?" Turner asked. "All this time?"

"For me I'm dark," Nancy explained. But this awkward way of putting it proved more than General Skelton could hear, even after three shoutings.

Turner Carmichael said, "We used to have this crazy colored girl who went around saying, 'I'se really white, 'cause all my chillun is,'" and of course *that* was what General Skelton picked to hear. "Party's getting rough," he complained.

"Granddaddy," Lorna cried, giggling, "you don't understand!"

"Don't I?" said the old gentleman. "Well, maybe I don't."

"Here, Nancy, come help me," said Lorna, leading her guest toward the kitchen.

On the way, Nancy heard Rob ask Turner, "Just where did you have this colored girl, did you say?"

"Don't be a dope. I said she worked for us."

"Aren't they a scream?" Lorna said, dragging a quart bottle of soda out of the refrigerator. "I thank God every night Granddaddy's deaf. You know, he was in the First World War and killed I don't know how many Germans, and he still can't stand to hear what he calls loose talk before a lady."

"I thought he was in the Civil War," said Nancy, and then of course she knew that that was the wrong thing and that Lorna, who just for an instant gave her a glance less than polite, was not going to forget it. The fact was, Nancy had never thought till that minute which war General Skelton had been in. She hadn't thought because she didn't care.

It had grown dark by now, and through the kitchen windows Nancy could see that the moon had risen—a moon in the clumsy stage, swelling between three-quarters and full, yet pouring out light on the water. Its rays were bursting against a long breakwater of concrete slabs, the remains of what the hurricane had shattered.

After saying such a fool thing, Nancy felt she could not stay in that kitchen another minute with Lorna, so she asked where she could go comb her hair. Lorna showed her down a hallway, kindly switching the lights on.

The Skeltons' bathroom was all pale blue and white, with handsome jars of rose bath salts and big fat scented bars of rosy soap. The lights came on impressively and the fixtures were heavy, yet somehow it all looked dead. It came to Nancy that she had really been wondering about just what would be in this sort of bathroom ever since she had seen those boys, with maybe Rob among them, playing tennis while she jumped on the trampoline. Surely the place had the air of an inner shrine, but what was there to see? The tops of all the bottles fitted firmly tight, and the soap in the tub was dry. Somebody had picked it all out—that was the point—judging soap and bath salts just the way they judged outsiders, business, real estate, politics. Nancy's father made judgments, too. Once, he argued all evening that Hitler was a well-meaning man; another time, he said the world was ready for the Communists. You could tell he was judging wrong, because he didn't have a bathroom like this one. Nancy's face in the mirror resembled a flower in a room that was too warm.

When she went out again, they had started dancing a little—a sort of friendly shifting around before the big glass windows overlooking the sound. General Skelton's chair was empty; he was gone. Down below, Lorna's parents could be heard coming in; her mother called upstairs. Her father appeared and shook hands all around. Mrs. Skelton soon followed him. He was wearing a white jacket, and she had on a silver cocktail dress with silver shoes. They looked like people in magazines. Mrs. Skelton held a crystal platter of things to eat in one hand, with a lace handkerchief pressed between the flesh and the glass in an inevitable sort of way.

In a moment, when the faces, talking and eating, the music, the talk, and the dancing swam to a still point before Nancy's eyes, she said, "You must all come to my house next week. We'll have a party."

A silence fell. Everyone knew where Nancy lived, in that little cluster of old run-down houses the boulevard swept by. They knew that her house, especially, needed paint outside and furniture inside. Her daddy drank too much, and through her dress they could perhaps clearly discern the pin that held her slip together. Maybe, since they knew everything, they could look right through the walls of the house and see her daddy's donkey.

"Sure we will," said Rob Acklen at once. "I think that would be grand."

"Sure we will, Nancy," said Lorna Skelton, who was such a good sport and who was not seeing Rob this summer.

"A party?" said Turner Carmichael, and swallowed a whole anchovy. "Can I come, too?"

Oh, dear Lord, Nancy was wondering, what made me say it? Then she was on the stairs with her knees shaking, leaving the party, leaving with Rob to go down to Biloxi, where the two of them always went, and hearing the right things said to her and Rob, and smiling back at the right things but longing to jump off into the dark as if it were water. The dark, with the moon mixed in with it, seemed to her like good deep water to go off in.

She might have known that in the Marine Room of the Buena Vista down in Biloxi, they would run into more friends of Rob's. They always ran into somebody, and she might have known. These particular ones had already arrived and were even waiting for Rob, being somewhat bored in the process. It wasn't that Rob was so bright and witty, but he listened and liked everybody; he saw them the way they liked to be seen. So then they would go on to new heights, outdoing themselves, coming to believe how marvellous they really were. Two fraternity brothers of his were there tonight. They were sitting at a table with their dates—two tiny girls with tiny voices, like mosquitoes. They at once asked Nancy where she went to college, but before she could reply and give it away that her school so far had been only a cow college up in Arkansas and that she had gone there because her daddy couldn't afford anywhere else, Rob broke in and answered for her. "She's been in a finishing school in Little Rock," he said, "but I'm trying to talk her into going to the university."

Then the girls and their dates all four spoke together. They said, "Great!"

"Now watch," said one of the little girls, whose name

was Teenie. "Cootie's getting out that little ole rush book."

Sure enough, the tiniest little notebook came out of the little cream silk bag of the other girl, who was called Cootie, and in it Nancy's name and address were written down with a sliver of a gold pencil. The whole routine was a fake, but a kind fake, as long as Rob was there. The minute those two got her into the ladies' room it would turn into another thing altogether; that she knew. Nancy knew all about mosquitoes. They'll sting me till I crumple up and die, she thought, and what will they ever care? So, when the three of them did leave the table, she stopped to straighten the strap of her shoe at the door to the ladies' room and let them go on through, talking on and on to one another about Rush Week. Then she went down a corridor and around a corner and down a short flight of steps. She ran down a long basement hallway where the service quarters were, past linen closets and cases of soft drinks, and, turning another corner and trying a door above a stairway, she came out, as she thought she would, in a night-club place called the Fishnet, far away in the wing. It was a good place to hide; she and Rob had been there often. I can make up some sort of story later, she thought, and crept up on the last barstool. Up above the bar, New Orleans-style (or so they said), a man was pumping tunes out of an electric organ. He wore rings on his chubby fingers and kept a handkerchief near him to mop his brow and to swab his triple chins with between songs. He waved his hand at Nancy. "Where's Rob, honey?" he asked.

She smiled but didn't answer. She kept her head back in the shadows. She wished only to be like another glass in the sparkling row of glasses lined up before the big gleam of mirrors and under the play of lights. What made me say that about a party, she kept wondering. To some people it would be nothing, nothing. But not to her. She fumbled in her bag for a cigarette. Inadvertently, she drank from a glass near her hand. The man sitting next to her smiled at her. "I didn't want it anyway," he said.

"Oh, I didn't mean—" she began. "I'll order one." Did you pay now? She rummaged in her bag.

But the man said "What'll it be?" and ordered for her. "Come on now, take it easy," he said. "What's your name?"

"Nothing," she said, by accident.

She had meant to say Nancy, but the man seemed to think it was funny. "Nothing what?" he asked. "Or is it by any chance Miss Nothing? I used to know a large family of Nothings, over in Mobile."

"Oh, I meant to say Nancy."

"Nancy Nothing. Is that it?"

Another teaser, she thought. She looked away from his eyes, which glittered like metal, and what she saw across the room made her uncertainties vanish. She felt her whole self settle and calm itself. The man she had seen that morning on the beach wearing a red bandanna shirt and shorts was standing near the back of the Fishnet, looking on. Now he was wearing a white dinner jacket and a black tie, with a red cummerbund over his large stomach, but he was unmistakably the same man. At that moment, he positively seemed to Nancy to be her own identity. She jumped up and left the teasing man at the bar and crossed the room.

"Remember me?" she said. "I saw you on the beach this morning."

"Sure I do. You ran off when it started to rain. I had to run, too."

"Why did you?" Nancy asked, growing happier every minute.

"Because the rain was so hot it burnt me. If I could roll up my sleeve, I'd show you the blisters on my arm."

"I believe you. I had some, too, but they went away." She smiled, and the man smiled back. The feeling was that they would be friends forever.

"Listen," the man said after a while. "There's a fellow here you've got to meet now. He's out on the veranda, because it's too hot in here. Anyway, he gets tired just with me. Now, you come on."

Nancy Lewis was always conscious of what she had left behind her. She knew that right now her parents and old Mrs. Poultney, with her rent collector's jaw, and Miss Henriette Dupré, with her religious calf eyes, and the Nattiers, mother and son, were all sitting on the back porch in the half-light, passing the bottle of 6-12 around, and probably right now discussing the fact that Nancy was out with Rob again. She knew that when her mother thought of Rob her heart turned beautiful and radiant as a seashell on a spring night. Her father, both at home and at his office, took his daughter's going out with Rob as a means of saying something disagreeable about Rob's father, who was a big insurance man. There was always some talk about how Mr. Acklen had trickily got out of the bulk of his hurricane-damage payments, the same as all the other insurance men had done. Nancy's mother was probably responding to such a charge at this moment. "Now, you don't know that's true," she would say. But old Mrs. Poultney would say she knew it was true with *her* insurance company (implying that she knew but wouldn't say about the Acklen company, too). Half the house she was renting to the Lewises had blown right off it—all one wing—and the upstairs bathroom was ripped in two, and you could see the wallpapered walls of all the rooms, and the bathtub, with its pipes still attached, had got blown into the telephone wires. If Mrs. Poultney had got what insurance money had been coming to her, she would have torn down this house and built a new one. And Mrs. Nattier would say that there was something terrible to her about seeing wallpapered rooms exposed that way. And Miss Henriette Dupré would say that the Dupré house had come through it all ab-so-lootly intact, meaning that the Duprés had been foresighted enough to get some sort of special heavenly insurance, and she would be just longing to embark on explaining how they came by it, and she would, too, given a tenth of a chance. And all the time this went on, Nancy could see into the Acklens' house just as clearly—see the Acklens sitting inside their sheltered game room after dinner, bathed in those soft bug-repellent lights. And what were the Acklens saying (along with their kind of talk about their kind of money) but that they certainly hoped Rob wasn't serious about that girl? Nothing had to matter if he wasn't serious. . . . Nancy could circle around all of them in her mind. She could peer into windows, overhearing; it was the only way she could look at people. No human in the whole human world seemed to her exactly made for her to stand in front of and look squarely in the eye, the way she could look Bernard Nattier in the eye (he not being a human, either) before taking careful aim to be sure not to miss him with a purseful of rocks and oyster shells, or the way she could look this big man in the red cummerbund in the eye, being convinced already that he was what her daddy called a "natural." Her daddy liked to come across people he could call that, because it made him feel superior.

As the big man steered her through the crowded room, threading among the tables, going out toward the veranda, he was telling her his life story all along the way. It seemed that his father was a terribly rich Yankee who paid him not to stay at home. He had been in love with a policeman's daughter from Pittsburgh, but his father broke it up. He was still in love with her and always would be. It was the way he was; he couldn't help being faithful, could he? His name was Alfred, but everybody called him Bub. The fellow his father paid to drive him around was right down there, he said, as they stepped through the door and out on the veranda.

Nancy looked down the length of the veranda, which ran along the side of the hotel, and there was a man sitting on a bench. He had on a white jacket and was staring straight ahead, smoking. The highway curled around the hotel grounds, following the curve of the shore, and the cars came glimmering past, one by one, sometimes with lights on inside, sometimes spilling radio music that trailed up in long waves and met the electric-organ music coming out of the bar. Nancy and Bub walked toward the man. Bub counselled her gently, "His name is Dennis." Some people in full evening dress were coming up the divided walk before the hotel, past the canna lilies blooming deeply red under the high, powerful lights, where the bugs coned in long footless whirlpools. The people were drunk and laughing.

"Hi, Dennis," Bub said. The way he said it, trying to sound confident, told her that he was scared of Dennis.

Dennis's head snapped up and around. He was an erect, strong, square-cut man, not very tall. He had put water on his light-brown hair when he combed it, so that it streaked light and dark and light again and looked like wood. He had cold eyes, which did not express anything—just the opposite of Rob Acklen's.

"What you got there?" he asked Bub.

"I met her this morning on the beach," Bub said.

"Been holding out on me?"

"Nothing like that," said Bub. "I just now saw her again."

The man called Dennis got up and thumbed his cigarette into the shrubbery. Then he carefully set his heels together and bowed. It was all a sort of joke on how he thought people here behaved. "Would you care to dance?" he inquired.

Dancing there on the veranda, Nancy noticed at once that he had a tense, strong wrist that bent back and forth like something manufactured out of steel. She also noticed that he was making her do whatever it was he called dancing; he was good at that. The music coming out of the Fishnet poured through the windows and around them. Dennis was possibly even thirty years old. He kept talking the whole time. "I guess he's told you everything, even about the policeman's daughter. He tells everybody every-thing, right in the first two minutes. I don't know if it's true, but how can you tell? If it wasn't true when it hap-pened, it is now." He spun her fast as a top, then slung her out about ten feet—she thought she would certainly sail right on out over the railing and maybe never stop till she landed in the gulf, or perhaps go splat on the high-way—but he got her back on the beat and finished up the thought, saying, "Know what I mean?"

"I guess so," Nancy said, and the music stopped.

The three of them sat down together on the bench.

"What do we do now?" Dennis asked.

"Let's ask her," said Bub. He was more and more de-lighted with Nancy. He had been tremendously encour-aged when Dennis took to her.

"You ask her," Dennis said.

"Listen, Nancy," Bub said. "Now, listen. Let me just tell you. There's so much money—that's the first thing to know. You've got no idea how much money there is. Really crazy. It's something, actually, that nobody knows—"

"If anybody knew," said Dennis, "they might have to tell the government."

"Anyway, my stepmother on this yacht in Florida, her own telephone—by radio, you know—she'd be crazy to meet you. My dad is likely off somewhere, but maybe not. And there's this plane down at Palm Beach, pilot and all, with nothing to do but go to the beach every day, just to pass away the time, and if he's not there for any reason, me and Dennis can fly just as good as we can drive. There's Alaska, Beirut—would you like to go to Beirut? I've always wanted to. There's anything you say."

"See that Cad out there?" said Dennis. "The yellow one with the black leather upholstery? That's his. I drive."

"So all you got to do," Bub told her, "is wish. Now, wait—now, think. It's important!" He all but held his hand over her mouth, as if playing a child's game, until finally he said, "Now! What would you like to do most in the world?"

"Go to New Orleans," said Nancy at once, "and eat some wonderful food."

"It's a good idea," said Dennis. "This dump is getting on my nerves. I get bored most of the time anyway, but today I'm bored silly."

"So wait here!" Nancy said. "So wait right here!"

She ran off to get Rob. She had all sorts of plans in her head.

But Rob was all taken up. There were now more of his friends. The Marine Room was full of people just like him, lounging around two big tables shoved together, with about a million 7-Up bottles and soda bottles and glasses before them, and girls spangled among them, all silver, gold, and white. It was as if while Nancy was gone they had moved into mirrors to multiply themselves. They were talking to themselves about things she couldn't join in, any more than you can dance without feet. Somebody was going into politics, somebody was getting married to a girl who trained horses, somebody was just back from Europe. The two little mosquito girls weren't saying anything much anymore; they had their little chins glued to their little palms. When anybody mentioned the university, it sounded like a small country the people right there were running *in absentia* to suit themselves. Last year's

Maid of Cotton was there, and so, it turned out, was the girl horse-trainer—tall, with a sheaf of upswept brown hair fastened with a glittering pin; she sat like the mast of a ship, smiling and talking about horses. Did she know personally every horse in the Southern states?

Rob scarcely looked up when he pulled Nancy in. "Where you been? What you want to drink?" He was having another good evening. He seemed to be sitting up above all the rest, as though presiding, but this was not actually so; only his fondness for every face he saw before him made him appear to be raised up a little, as if on a special chair.

And, later on, it seemed to Nancy that she herself had been, among them, like a person who wasn't a person—another order of creature passing among or even through them. Was it just that nothing, nobody, could really distract them when they got wrapped up in themselves?

"I met some people who want to meet you," she whispered to Rob. "Come on out with me."

"O.K.," he said. "In a minute. Are they from around here?"

"Come on, come on," she urged. "Come on out."

"In a minute," he said. "I will in a minute," he promised.

Then someone noticed her pulling at his sleeve, and she thought she heard Lorna Skelton laugh.

She went racing back to Bub and Dennis, who were waiting for her so docilely they seemed to be the soul of goodness, and she said, "I'll just ride around for a while, because I've never been in a Cadillac before." So they rode around and came back and sat for a while under the huge brilliant overhead lights before the hotel, where the bugs spiralled down. They did everything she said. She could make them do anything. They went to three different places, for instance, to find her some Dentyne, and when they found it they bought her a whole carton of it.

The bugs did a jagged frantic dance, trying to climb high enough to kill themselves, and occasionally a big one crashed with a harsh dry sound against the pavement. Nancy remembered dancing in the open air, and the rough salt feel of the air whipping against her skin as she spun fast against the air's drift. From behind she heard the resonant, constant whisper of the gulf. She looked toward the hotel doors and thought that if Rob came through she would hop out of the car right away, but he didn't come. A man she knew passed by, and she just all of a sudden said, "Tell Rob I'll be back in a minute," and he, without even looking up, said, "O.K., Nancy," just like it really was O.K., so she said what the motor was saying, quiet but right there, and definitely running just under the splendid skin of the car, "Let's go on for a little while."

"Nancy, I think you're the sweetest girl I ever saw," said Bub, and they drove off.

She rode between them, on the front seat of the Cadillac. The top was down and the moon spilled over them as they rode, skimming gently but powerfully along the shore and the sound, like a strong rapid cloud travelling west. Nancy watched the point where the moon actually met the water. It was moving and still at once. She thought that it was glorious, in a messy sort of way. She would have liked to poke her head up out of the water right there. She could feel the water pouring back through her white-blond hair, her face slathering over with moonlight.

"If it hadn't been for that crazy rain," Bub kept saying, "I wouldn't have met her."

"Oh, shut up about that goofy rain," said Dennis.

"It was like being spit on from above," said Nancy.

The needle crept up to eighty or more, and when they had left the sound and were driving through the swamp Nancy shivered. They wrapped her in a lap robe from the back seat and turned the radio up loud.

It was since she got back, since she got back home from New Orleans, that her mother did not put on the thin voile afternoon dress anymore and serve iced tea to the neighbors on the back porch. Just yesterday, having nothing to do in the hot silence but hear the traffic stream by on the boulevard, and not wanting a suntan and being certain the telephone would not ring, Nancy had taken some lemonade over to Bernard Nattier, who was sick in bed with the mumps. He and his mother had one room between them, over at Mrs. Poultney's house, and they had stacks of magazines—the *Ladies' Home Journal*, *McCall's*, *Life*, and *Time*—piled along the walls. Bernard lay on a bunk bed pushed up under the window, in all the close heat, with no breeze able to come in at all. His face was puffed out and his eyes feverish. "I brought you some lemonade," said Nancy, but he said he couldn't drink it because it hurt his gums. Then he smiled at her, or tried to—it must have hurt even to do that, and it certainly made him look silly, like a cartoon of himself, but it was sweet.

"I love you, Nancy," he said, most irresponsibly.

She thought she would cry. She had honestly tried to kill him with those rocks and oyster shells. He knew that very well, and he, from the moment he had seen her, had set out to make her life one long torment, so where could it come from, a smile like that, and what he said? She didn't know. From the fever, maybe. She said she loved him, too.

Then, it was last night, just the night before, that her father had got drunk and made speeches beginning "To think that a daughter of mine . . ." Nancy had sat through it all crouched in the shadows on the stair landing, in the very spot where the moss or old seaweed back of the panelling smelled the strongest and dankest, and thought of her mother upstairs, lying, clothed, straight out on the bed in the dark, with a headache and no cover on and maybe the roof above her melted away. Nancy looked down to where her father was marching up to the donkey that said, "If you really want to look like me—Just keep right on talking," and was picking it up and throwing it down, right on the floor. She cried out, before she knew it—"Oh!"—seeing him do the very thing she had so often meant to do herself. Why had he? Why? Because the whiskey had run out on him? Or because he had got too much of it again? Or from trying to get in one good lick at everything there was? Or because the advice he loved so much seemed now being offered to him?

But the donkey did not break. It lay there, far down in the tricky shadows; Nancy could see it lying there, looking back over its shoulder with its big red grinning mouth, and teeth like piano keys, still saying the same thing, naturally. Her father was tilting uncertainly down toward it, unable, without falling flat on his face, to reach it. This made a problem for him, and he stood thinking it all over, taking every aspect of it well into account, even though the donkey gave the impression that not even with a sledgehammer would it be broken, and lay as if on some deep distant sea floor, toward which all the sediment of life was drifting, drifting, forever slowly down. . . .

Beirut! It was the first time she had remembered it. They had said they would take her there, Dennis and Bub, and then she had forgotten to ask, so why think of it right now, on the street uptown, just when she saw Rob Acklen coming along? She would have to see him sometimes, she guessed, but what did Beirut have to do with it?

"Nancy Lewis," he said pleasantly, "you ran out on me. Why did you act like that? I was always nice to you."

"I told them to tell you," she said. "I just went to ride around for a while."

"Oh, I got the word, all right. About fifty different people saw you drive off in that Cadillac. Now about a hundred claim to have. Seems like everybody saw those two characters but me. What did you do it for?"

"I didn't like those Skeltons, all those people you knew. I didn't like those sorority girls, that Teenie and Cootie. You knew I didn't, but you always took me where they were just the same."

"But the point is," said Rob Acklen, "I thought you liked me."

"Well, I did," said Nancy Lewis, as though it all had happened a hundred years ago. "Well, I did like you just fine."

They were talking on the street still. There had been the tail of a storm that morning, and the palms were blowing. There was a sense of them streaming like green flags above the low town.

Rob took Nancy to the drugstore and sat at a booth with her. He ordered her a fountain Coke and himself a cup of coffee. "What's happened to you?" he asked her.

She realized then, from what he was looking at, that something she had only half noticed was certainly there to be seen—her skin, all around the edges of her white blouse, was badly bruised and marked, and there was the purplish mark on her cheekbone she had more or less powdered over, along with the angry streak on her neck.

"You look like you fell through a cotton gin," Rob Acklen continued, in his friendly way. "You're not going to say the rain over in New Orleans is just scalding hot, are you?"

"I didn't say anything," she returned.

"Maybe the mosquitoes come pretty big over there," he suggested. "They wear boxing gloves, for one thing, and, for another—"

"Oh, stop it, Rob," she said and wished she was anywhere else.

It had all stemmed from the moment down in the French Quarter, over late drinks somewhere, when Dennis had got nasty enough with Bub to get rid of him, so that all of Dennis's attention from that point onward had gone exclusively to Nancy. This particular attention was relentless and direct, for Dennis was about as removed from any sort of affection and kindness as a human could be. Maybe it had all got boiled out of him; maybe he had never had much to get rid of. What he had to say to her was nothing she hadn't heard before, nothing she hadn't already been given more or less to understand from mosquitoes, people, life-in-general, and the rain out of the sky. It was just that he said it in a final sort of way—that was all.

"I was in a wreck," said Nancy.

"Nobody killed, I hope," said Rob.

She looked vaguely across at Rob Acklen with pretty, dark-blue eyes that seemed to be squinting to see through shifting lights down in the deep sea; for in looking at him, in spite of all he could do, she caught a glimmering impression of herself, of what he thought of her, of how soft her voice always was, her face like a warm flower.

"I was doing my best to be nice to you. Why wasn't that enough?"

"I don't know," she said.

"None of those people you didn't like were out to get you. They were all my friends."

When he spoke in this handsome, sincere, and democratic way, she had to agree; she had to say she guessed that was right.

Then he said, "I was having such a good summer. I imagined you were, too," and she thought, He's coming down deeper and deeper, but one thing is certain—if he gets down as far as I am, he'll drown.

"You better go," she told him, because he had said he was on his way up to Shreveport on business for his father. And because Bub and Dennis were back; she'd seen them drift by in the car twice, once on the boulevard and once in town, silenter than cloud, Bub in the back, with his knees propped up, reading a magazine.

"I'll be going in a minute," he said.

"You just didn't realize I'd ever go running off like that," Nancy said, winding a damp Coca-Cola straw around her finger.

"Was it the party, the one you said you wanted to give? You didn't have to feel—"

"I don't remember any party," she said quickly.

Her mother lay with the roof gone, hands folded. Nancy felt that people's mothers, like wallpapered walls after a hurricane, should not be exposed. Her father at last successfully reached the donkey, but he fell in the middle of the rug, while Nancy, on the stair landing, smelling seaweed, asked herself how a murderous child with swollen jaws happened to mention love, if love is not a fever, and the storm-driven sea struck the open reef and went roaring skyward, splashing a tattered gull that clutched at the blast—but if we will all go there immediately it is safe in the Dupré house, because they have this holy candle. There are hidden bone-cold lairs no one knows of, in rock beneath the sea. She shook her bone-white hair.

Rob's whole sensitive face tightened harshly for saying what had to come next, and she thought for a while he wasn't going to make it, but he did. "To hell with it. To absolute hell with it then." He looked stricken, as though he had managed nothing but damaging himself.

"I guess it's just the way I am," Nancy murmured. "I just run off sometimes."

Her voice faded in a deepening glimmer where the human breath is snatched clean away and there are only bubbles, iridescent and pure. When she dove again, they rose in a curving track behind her.

Judith Kane

It must have been Thursday when I first came to Mrs. Holloway's and certainly it was June. It had to be Thursday because the first three days of the week I was busy working for that professor, typing his thesis notes, checking his sources, and keeping his office in order. It wasn't Friday because I wanted to settle in my new quarters before the weekend, when somebody might ask me to the movies or a party or something. I know absolutely that it was June, because that was when the summer term began at the university. Since my dormitory had closed for lack of students to stay in it, I had to find somewhere off campus to stay.

A Thursday in June. Sometime in the late 'thirties. Money was all-important. A dollar was a dollar. The professor I worked for was paying me, and by working hard on my own I could get a couple of courses ticked off and my family wouldn't have to keep me in school quite so long. Times were hard and everyone had to work to get ahead. My education had to be given me somehow, but I must understand that because of it my sisters were going around in hand-me-down clothes, the house needed a coat of paint, and the fence was falling down. I knew it all, in all its earnest truth and rightness, and had willingly put my nineteen-year-old girl-shoulder to the wheel where it belonged; yet I was sulky, too. In those pre-war days, going to summer school was something like a reformatory sentence or having to get a job as a waitress.

Having paid the cab, I stood on the curb for a good long minute or so in my limp dirndl skirt and white blouse, dirty from moving things out of the dormitory closet, with suitcases beside me on the grass along with grocery store cartons filled with odds and ends, coathangers tied together by the hooks, my old rag doll, and patchwork pillows stuffed around some books on the English Renaissance. It was afternoon and the sun was straight in my eyes as I shielded my face with one hand and looked at the house I was coming to take a room in, a large three-storey white frame house with verandas and balconies, turret and shade tree, holes neatly bored in every step to let the rainwater through, and wrought-iron footscraper clamped to the floor right by the fresh hemp doormat. Mrs. Holloway's house on Knowlton Place.

The maid let me in, helping me get everything upstairs, trudging good-naturedly with me time after time through the hot front yard into the cooler interior where I was cheered by a renewed vision of built-in columned fireplace with mirror set above, glassed-in bookcases in dark-stained oak, dark-banistered staircase with a creaking step or two and a cool pitcher of lemonade set out on the landing. I had remembered all this from the time I came to see the room and take it; now I found it all the same. I sat on the bed in my small front room before unpacking, comforted by the hominess of Mrs. Holloway's. A breeze blew through the windows, which overlooked the street. It touched my hot brow and damp hair.

It's better than the dormitory, I thought. *There could be worse places, even if I don't want to go to summer school.*

A door must have closed in the hallway behind me, but I didn't hear it. My own door was open, and I felt a presence behind me and turned around with a start.

"Just moved in?"

Looks like it, I would have cracked to anybody I knew. Instead, I nodded politely, then did a real double take. The girl who was standing there was somebody I knew and had known for a long time. She didn't know me at all. The only reason I knew her was the same reason everybody knew her: she was so beautiful, tall and put together like a Greek statue, with cornsilk hair brushed back and hanging or drawn up in a swirl behind. The boys all talked about her for obvious reasons, admiring her and wishing they had a chance to date her and all; and the girls all wanted to look like her. Now, there she stood, at closer range than I had ever seen her, in a loose blue housecoat, just out of the shower, with the air of someone who had been here in this house a long time.

"Judith Kane!" I said. "I didn't know you lived here."

"I thought I was going to be alone all summer," she said. "Everybody left but me."

"You just about will be," I said, "except on weekends. I've got so much work to do I expect I may even have to sleep in the library."

"I used to work there," she said, "after I graduated."

"What do you do now?" I asked, after telling her my

name and who I worked for. I was hardly conscious of what words I was using, her looks were so astonishing. I know all this about how they say Southern girls are so pretty and how they come pouring out of little towns and from way up in the hills to get elected Miss Pickle Queen and Miss Watermelon Queen, Miss Centennial Year, Miss America, Maid of Cotton, Miss Universe, and so on. All true, but not all that interesting. Nothing of this related to Judith Kane. She wasn't cute or pretty, her measurements weren't for contests or advertising copy, but for aesthetics; she was, simply, a creation.

"Do?" she repeated. "Not much of anything, I guess. That's just the trouble. Welcome, anyway. I'd help you unpack but don't have time."

The reason she didn't have time was because she had a date. I soon heard the front door close and by going to the window to look could see her go off across the street with a lean, sandy-haired guy, who moved out beside her to where a blue-green Pontiac convertible stood shimmering beside the curb. The doors went *chunk* and *chunk* and the car accelerated silently like a lioness which has sighted the prey. Judith's white shoes, her lime-green summer dress and scrolled-up hair had made me feel the way I looked, tired and unattractive. I had sat brooding the whole time she was dressing. Whoever came to take me somewhere, any fool could plainly see, was bound to get interested in her. I felt I had no looks or clothes or any asset to hold a candle to hers. Personally speaking, the prospects of this summer didn't give me a lot to rave about.

But, as the days went by, I saw I had been hasty, at least as regards Judith Kane.

Judith was twenty-four, that was the first thing to cheer me. Though to admit to being that old seemed a shame, she evidently didn't mind, for Mrs. Holloway knew it and told me. "Not that it's any of my business," she said, giving me my mail. "All I wonder is what's she still doing around here, not going to school or anything." The boys who came around sometimes on weekends to take me to the movies seemed able to survive the sight of her after all. One said she was a knockout all right, and let it go at that; another said he'd heard she was expensive. She was friendly with them in a harmless, open way, and might run up from the basement in an old skirt with a scarf around her head and some warm ironing over her arm, making no effort to please anybody. She told me once in passing that boys without money were of no interest to her. I guess the boy with that Pontiac must have had financial resources, all right. Seen close to, I found him not so much attractive as well turned-out. The possession of the right articles meant a lot to him—you could tell that by the way he opened the car door—and Judith said he had good taste. Once he brought her a bottle of champagne and they sat down on Mrs. Holloway's front porch in the swing drinking it. She poured out some in a fruit juice glass from the kitchen and ran upstairs to give it to me. "It's champagne," she said. "Take some." I was under a reading lamp, bent over a book with my hair in pins. *This is not the way to drink champagne*, I thought, and finished it off like Alka-Seltzer. The boy's name was Grant Exum, I now remember, and somebody in summer school mentioned him one day, again in connection with his car, which was the fanciest thing around, and further said that he wanted to marry Judith Kane, but his parents wouldn't let him marry anybody till he finished law school. "Money families," whoever was telling this remarked, "are always bossy. Po' folks are a whole lot easier." The memory drifts back after so many years: sitting out gossiping in a group on the library steps, with sun glossing the empty summer campus, far and wide.

I then concluded that Judith stayed around on account of Grant Exum, holding a job downtown in a small branch library which, with summer hours, took up scarcely half her time. It could not have paid her very much or interested her very much. In the afternoons I came in from work, toiling up the stairs to my room, she would generally have been home for an hour or so, and would be reading out in the corridor, where a breeze drew, smoking a cigarette with her hair up, or sometimes sipping some of Mrs. Holloway's lemonade. She seldom said anything, and often never even looked up: it was rather like passing a garden statue, and it became disconcerting only when she did speak. To hear "Hi, there" or "How's it going?" was almost as startling as her first appearance had been. She read T. S. Eliot, Auden, Mann, Proust—a lot of highbrow things—with concentration, paying that close sort of attention that does not seem to have enjoyment or future conversation anywhere in mind, the matter being more urgent than that. I was in literature, too, but might as well have been analyzing Tennessee rainwater for all she would care to talk to me about. But I finally came to realize, the first couple of weeks having gone by like this, that Judith Kane's life, like her extraordinary looks, was no more to me than Mrs. Holloway's, or the house which had somehow managed to absorb both of them into it; for if the downstairs with its starched antimacassars and glass-front bookshelves and sanded-glass ornaments belonged to Mrs. Holloway, the upstairs—white-curtained, smooth, simple, immaculate, and quiet—had long been Judith's, and hers was the rocking chair that I, finding it empty in the hallway, dropped into one afternoon when I arrived home early from work.

The heat was severe that summer. I watched the white curtains swell and thought that I was tired thinking of anything that came out of books or went into them. I thought I would be glad to think of nothing, for one whole year at least. But all I had ahead were a few free weeks in August and September before the round began again. And there was still some of July and August yet to go.

I heard Judith come in, stop for the mail and start upstairs, and I lingered, rocking and comfortable in the afternoon breeze, before getting up to go to my room and give her favorite place to her, as obviously I had no business there. But rounding the landing and seeing me, she made a gesture that indicated I should stay where I was, and as a further surprise, sat down on the edge of the cot Mrs. Holloway kept out in the hallway and offered me a cigarette, lighting one for herself. She had on a white linen dress with sea horses worked on the front in dark brilliant thread. I never saw a dress like it, before or since.

"Do you want to hear a story?" she began. "I feel I've just got to tell somebody, I don't know why. It happened last spring—you won't tell? That's a stupid thing to ask. What I mean is, if you tell, get it right and don't make it sound silly."

The remark revealed nothing so much as how she thought of me—not me so much personally, I believed, as girls of my average sort—but being curious, I decided not to object. At that point I would have listened to anyone's story, to anything at all that didn't come out of a book.

It had happened one early morning back in the spring, before I had moved in. There were only some elderly ladies across from her, now graduated from a teachers' college nearby and gone back to wherever they came from, no one in the front rooms but an occasional overnight guest. Judith had been standing in her own room at the window looking down on the little garden of the tall brown house next door, wearing nothing and brushing her hair. It was then she felt suddenly drawn, compelled, to look up instead of down and saw in the attic window above a young man leaning close to the glass and watching her. He was sprawled face down on a bed or bunk and his face wore the expression of one who breathes the air of paradise. She had the distinct feeling that he was exactly where he always spent this hour of the morning, had been there not once, not twice or a dozen times, but morning after morning for perhaps a year, perhaps for the entire three years she had lived there.

"But do you always," I asked her, "stand there without any clothes on and brush your hair? Even in the winter?"

"I guess I do, quite a lot. Yes, I hadn't thought of it so

much—but I did for a long time make a habit of it. I don't go near that window now, and as he saw me look up that time he hasn't been back either—at least, I've never seen him. I've not seen him even on this street again since that day."

"Well, who is he?" I asked her. "Did you recognize him?"

To me this all seemed rather funny and I almost laughed, but at this point she became terribly serious and tried twice to go on but her voice, so much in control ordinarily that it seemed a cool comment on anything that could possibly be brought up, like a water sprinkler passing over a lawn, faded out twice when she tried to speak. She essayed another cigarette, but her hands shook so violently, she had to give up.

"I saw him today." She finally got it out. Her anguish at this point was so intense it got across to me something of the force the experience had had for her. I began to feel uneasily that I might have done better to stick to books.

"I've got to tell somebody," she went on. "I've felt for months that I was losing my mind. I couldn't see myself in a psychiatrist's office; in the first place, can't afford it. I began to see that boy's face everywhere—carhops, movie ushers, students on the bus, taxi drivers—for a while, every face could make me look at it at a certain distance, but once the distance lessened and it wouldn't be that face, after all, I would get a sick dizzy feeling, and wild . . . wild!" She laughed. "There was a shoe clerk once . . . But it's no use remembering them all. A lot of stupid pick-ups, when they noticed. Somebody to get rid of."

"But," I said, though I hesitated to become practical,

"wouldn't it have been simple just to go next door and ask who the boy was—or maybe get somebody to do it for you?"

She hardly heard me, remarking after a long silence, "I did go there once. Nobody was in, but the door was open. So I went all the way upstairs, up to the attic. There's only that one room plus a nightmarish kind of storage place, trunks and old pictures, a box full of tennis stuff, a rack of old dresses and suits. He isn't there any more, nobody is. Nobody saw me. I went there and came back here and then wondered if I dreamed it all. I wondered if I was dreaming when I came back and was actually still up in that attic. And next I wondered if I were both places and could look down at myself, in my own room."

"Good Lord," I said, and saw there wasn't any end to thoughts like that. "But you saw him. You said you met him today."

"He crossed the street by the grill and I was coming out, so we met."

"Then what happened?"

"His name is Yancey Clements. He teaches swimming and gym at the Y. On weekends he keeps the desk there. Sometimes he works at a high-school gym over in the east of the city. He used to be a paper boy."

At the end of this recital, I broke out laughing, but she did not hear me laugh. She had turned pale and her make-up seemed to be too strong for her face. Crazy as it all might sound to me, it had succeeded in stirring her as ordinary things did not.

"So did you talk to him?" I asked.

"Oh, he knew right away why I stopped him. I felt he understood everything in a minute, even before I spoke or got across the street with him. He said he'd moved from that house. I think he decided to move the day I looked up. Then he said he wouldn't see me."

"So that finishes that," I said.

"It doesn't finish anything. Why do you think that? I begged him. Indeed I did. Finally, he gave in. He's going to have a drink with me, tonight, and we'll talk, something will happen to break it up for me. I've got to break it up, you see. It's got into everything."

She had wandered nervously about the cot, and had reached the pair of windows through which the breeze was now blowing more strongly. The white sheer curtains, standing out, blew around her, and she looked hectic and for the first time I thought this house could not really contain her, a big friendly old comfortable innocent house like this. She was threatening it already, and had been for a long time.

Singular though it was, I for some reason did not mention this conversation to anyone for a time, nor did I receive any further confidence from Judith. I did not for one thing, see her, even in passing. At the weekend she went off early with the law student in the Pontiac and did not reappear till Monday.

When I finally talked about her, it was to a graduate student named Scott Crawford—older even than twenty-four, I guess—who worked near me in the library and sometimes asked me over to the grill for coffee, or across from the campus to a café for a beer. This time, evening

being nearly on us, it was across the street we went, and
that was how I happened to come out with it all. It would
have been surprising if I hadn't, though, for I had been
confiding just about everything I had on my mind to Scott
Crawford, for about a year now, and he talked a lot to me
too, seeming to enjoy it, for we used to laugh a lot together.

"So what happened when she saw him?" he asked me.

"Well, I don't know yet," I said.

"It's funny your telling me," he said.

"Well," I said, "I knew you knew her slightly."

"Slightly! What gave you that impression? I used to go
with her."

"I didn't know that."

"I was never so in love in my life."

"I didn't know that either," I said.

"I know you didn't, or you wouldn't have mentioned
her current problem, I don't think. At least, not in the
way you did, like a curious thing. It is a curious thing. But
once you understand her tendencies, then it gets pretty
clear. She broke everything off with me. Reason? She
couldn't see herself as a professor's wife in some pokey little college town. She has this idea about herself, about her
own image. Being intelligent and looking like that, I guess
you think it's just a happy miracle. Well, maybe it ought
to be a happy miracle, but how is she not to realize it?
And realizing it, how is she not to ask herself the main
question: What's good enough? What's great enough?
What could possibly be good or great enough for Judith
Kane? Not that she'd come right out with it, nothing
blunt or corny. But if she doesn't say it to herself, she's

letting the mirror say it, forty times a day. Do I think she was right to give me up? Sure, I think she was right. I agree with her."

I had to grin a little because he said this last in the self-amused way he had, half-bitterness, half-gaiety, that made him engaging and showed his intelligence to me much more than the doctor's dissertation he was slaving over, trying to get it done before school was out, so he could qualify for a higher salary somewhere. I would probably never read it anyway. Scott Crawford smoked a pipe and carried masses of stuff around with him, to stoke it and clean it and light it and so on. He worked on this pipe as hard as some men work on cars. Picking all his junk off the table took about five minutes at the least, and during all this time he thought steadily on about the state of affairs at Mrs. Holloway's.

I, meantime, thought on about him, about what I knew of him, that is. He lived near the East campus, two blocks over toward the park, in an apartment with thin walls and sprung furniture. His wife was rather pretty but had begun to look tired of the life there. Her heart was set on having a house someday. He sometimes asked a few of us over to have a beer and talk about things. The baby had cried with a heat rash the last time I was there. That was June, I remembered, thinking it must by now be about melted away like a snail, but he said it was all right. That he was attractive, everyone agreed; though that he was completely unconcerned about it, all could see. He was respected by the faculty, and I once overheard a professor say that he had a classical, unsentimental mind. He spoke with a harsh, back-country *R*, almost like a Yankee, and

this gave a clean, intellectual turn to his speech, and drew
the kind of attention to it that clarity always commands.

That night, when we got out on the street where the
evening was still coming slowly on through the lingering
heat from pavement and grass, I could still sense the direction of his thoughts, like seeing the segment of a path.
"No good will come of it," he said, and shook himself together for going back to the library and getting down to
his grind. As we approached a parting of ways within the
library foyer, he threw an arm around me. "Look, honey,
you find out what happened, hear?"

I didn't say I would or wouldn't, just ran up the steps
away from him, wishing I'd never mentioned Judith Kane.
Had she confided in me because she had learned somehow
that I knew Scott Crawford? I wondered. Whether the
answer was yes or no, I just was not going to go into it
any further, just as I was not going to conclude that Scott
had married his wife Ruth on the rebound, or let it interest
me in the least that he was never going to be really happy
now. Having been so terribly, gorgeously, deeply in love
with Judith. What business was it of mine? I had wasted
time over there talking and would have to work till ten instead of nine. I ran down the hall to plunge into a mass of
stacked up carbons on onionskin with footnotes two-thirds
the way up every page, and ran smack into my professor,
who had come back over for a book.

"What's the matter with you?" he asked.

"Nothing," I said, breathing beer upon him, without a
doubt.

"Must be good," he said, an automatic phrase. He never
really noticed anything that wasn't down in print.

What he was working on was a treatise on Hawthorne's ideas of good and evil. He kept me working along with him to verify footnotes and I had to wade through a lot of old musty New England sermons, too, copying out parts that might have some bearing on his train of thought. The odd thing was that this man seemed so mild and inattentive—he could never get my name straight—I wondered if he ever would have thought there was any such thing as good and evil if he hadn't come across the words in books. Ideas did excite him, though. He once came in just bursting with something which had come to him while walking past the grill, namely, that the great white squid in "Moby Dick" might have been deliberately used by Melville to symbolize love and goodness, just as the white whale was nemesis and evil. He was heatedly explaining this to me, and I couldn't help but think what his wife had to listen to while cooking supper. "A squid?," I said. "You mean those awful things like octopuses?" It sort of took the wind out of his sails, putting it that way.

I chose to ignore Scott Crawford's request to check up on Judith Kane. Wouldn't that have made me more of a go-between than ever? I didn't want to be one.

Then one late middle of the night I woke and couldn't sleep, the heat was so intense and not a breath of air was stirring. The sheet stuck to my back, and I could hear the tap drip from the kitchen downstairs, and somewhere way off a motor grinding, trying to start on a rundown battery. I got up to run water over my wrists and put a wet cloth on the back of my neck and do all the other little things they cheerfully advise in the newspaper columns

when you're stifling to death, and when I went through
the hall past the cot and rocking chair there sat Judith,
smoking.

"Sit down," she said. "We'll whisper. Have a cigarette."

"It's not only too hot to smoke; it's too hot to breathe,"
I said.

"True," she said, lighting a fresh one off the stub.

"So what happened?" I asked her. "Did you see the
gym teacher?"

"He didn't come. I looked him up the next day at the Y
and he just got angry. He said he didn't come because he
didn't want to."

"So he was just a peeper and starer, after all," I said.
Why couldn't she stop it?

"I don't believe it," she answered at once, with the
quickness of anger, or fear. "I don't believe that for a
minute."

"But isn't he a lot younger than—" I paused, "younger
than we are?"

"Oh, sure." She laughed in a hushed clear way, and
seemed in such a perfectly good humor with herself I
couldn't think but that another person was suffering like
this somewhere and she was describing it all. "I wasn't
considering matrimony," she said. "He knows how I feel;
he knows it all. He just doesn't care. He saw me as I am,
and he does not care. It's all I can hear, all the time. A
voice inside, on a record as big as the moon. Would you
like to live like that?"

"I'd stop it," I said. "Shut it off."

"How?"

"Just do it," I said. "Do it anyway."

"I can't," she said. "I just can't."

She did look, even in the dark, terribly thin. She had begun to look like a *Vogue* model. I asked then if she still had her job—she said she had given it up. I wondered what she was living on, but guessed she hadn't eaten anything in days and did nothing but smoke, read, and drink lemonade. The law student had called about a million times, but she never would come to the phone, and even he had given up. She made me think there must be times when the world is separated from yourself with something like a wall of glass that you cannot find a foothold on, and what if the key to the one gate in it is in the possession of something which calls itself Yancey Clements and works at the Y?

"Just to talk to him would make me feel better," she said, in a calmer tone. "He won't even do that. I'm a mass of neuroses," she laughed, "and everything I do or think is in a world by itself and can't get out."

"Maybe you ought to just try going out and eating a lot of good food," I suggested. "Starting with breakfast in the morning."

She seemed to give me up, and snuffing out her final cigarette, wadding the pack for hurling in the wastebasket, she started back to her room. "What's it to you?" she asked, good-humoredly, as always. "What should it be to you?"

Her door closed, and I had never once mentioned Scott Crawford. I had clammed up dead to the world around his name.

The next morning Mrs. Holloway stopped me at the door. She wanted to know what on earth was the matter with Judith. Was she sick? If so, why not see a doctor? She had taken her chance, when Judith was in the bath one day, to peek into that room, and could hardly see anything through smoke so thick it looked like a gambling house. There were choked ash trays islanded around and shoals of books, and the bed looked to have had a wild cat in it. I said I didn't know anything about it, I was always working. But I had heard the mounting anxiety in her voice and knew her mild, widowed world was being shaken, trembling like a great big web that's all carefully worked out to hold in every part. Next thing the house would shake, for they'd be at each other in some final way.

After lunch I went over to the Y and asked for Yancey Clements. They said he wasn't working there right now, but was out doing some sort of gym teaching or other in a high school in the east of the city. That was how I happened to be on the bus in the early afternoon heat riding to a strange part of town where they had, miraculously, tiny friendly houses with small front yards, small plots of flowers, windows open, radios going. How nice, I kept thinking. How nice it is.

The high school, a large, dark-brick building, was summer-empty. From the gym, way out in the back wing, I heard somebody bouncing a basketball. There was the usual acrid smell, the deep thumbed-book smells, chalk, blackboards, erasers, and floor polish smells, but all breathed over and subdued by summer, and back near the gym door, overriding everything, were the sweat smells of basketball uniforms, along with the sound of the ball spanking harder and harder in the silence of the building. I

was sure the boy with the basketball would turn out to be
Yancey Clements, but I was wrong.

He was only a stringy high-school boy in a moth-eaten
red jersey and blue trunks too big for him, whamming the
ball at the floor as though he'd never done another thing in
his life. I thought I would have to go and take the ball
away from him to get his attention, but he finally looked
up. "I'm looking for Yancey Clements," I said, or shouted,
over the sound of the ball. "Is he here, or not?" The boy
jerked his head. Then Yancey himself stepped out of a
small dark doorway that led back of the stands into the
lockers, beyond a doubt.

I knew right away this really was Yancey because I had
seen him, I now realized, from time to time at the ham-
burger place near the Y. He must have just showered and
dressed because he had on a pair of old cotton trousers and
a clean white shirt. He was blond with a shock of hair
that came up like a rooster's comb, and he had a very
funny face, with protuberant teeth that crossed each other
in front, a high bridged nose, and grey-blue eyes. He was
absolutely humorless and he came straight to me before I
could speak and said, "Don't think I don't know why
you're here."

Good Lord, I thought, *he thinks I'm after him, too.*

"Listen, you come on over with me," he said. "I was
just going for a Coke."

We crossed the street, which was empty, and sat down
in the drugstore. He ordered Cokes for both of us, and
when they came he stuck a pair of straws in his bottle, and
then did the same for me, in the manner of one making an
enormous concession, and behaving like a gentleman if it

killed him. "I prefer a glass with ice in it," I almost said, but not wanting to throw him into a rage, I let it go.

"That girl is nuts," he said. "I don't care about seeing her. I told her that. I just don't care. She's beautiful, but she's nuts. Look at the trouble I've gone to. You think I like living over here? I couldn't stay over there and have her hanging around, that's a positive fact."

"But look," I said, "I'm sure she'd be different from what you think if you'd only talk to her. She might be reasonable and very sweet, and get over it all just over a Coke in the drugstore—like this, for instance. What harm would there be in trying? She laughs about it all herself," I added.

"Oh, she does?"

"You did start it," I said. "And now she feels awful. If only you were a little kind—"

"Kind!" He bit his lip stubbornly; he was nervous and tough, and no one should have said "kind" to him.

I rode back on the bus; I was the only person on it besides the bus driver and a colored maid who rode only four stops, and looked out the window the whole time, daydreaming. It was when we got on the long hill going from one side of the city to the other (and what with very little traffic at that hour of the afternoon, the bus went flying along, reeling, bounding and rattling over the rough uneven brick and asphalt) that all the colored beads began to fall off my hat. It was an old hat, and I had found it in the college office where I worked, having left it there after church last Easter. It was the only hat I owned; I had had it since high school. It was navy blue straw with a bunch of large vari-colored glass beads sewed on the band, and it

went with everything and was never out of style and
showed no age at all except that I had often in moments of
stress reached up and twisted the wire which threaded the
beads together, and I must undoubtedly have twisted it
several times that day or else the wire had about died of
old age, because every time the bus hit another bump in
the road another bead fell off on the floor. They made a
terrible racket rolling and tumbling around, and as the hill
was steep, several rolled all the way down the aisle and up
around the driver's feet. He stopped the bus at the bottom
of the hill. "Listen, Miss," he said, "do you want these
things?"

"Well, no, I guess not," I said. It just seemed like too
much trouble; and besides, how would I get them back
on? He began to pick them up anyway.

"I thought at first you were throwing them," he said.
"There were some kids in here, throwing some marbles
the other day. One or two people tripped up on them.
Them things," he said, "are worse'n banana peel, and if you
think of old people and all . . ."

"I wasn't throwing anything," I said. "It was an accident."

That night I saw Scott Crawford, or rather he saw me.
He came all the way over to my office in the library
where I had to work that evening to make up for the
afternoon.

"How is Judith?" he asked me. We had gone out to sit
on the steps of the library by then, and it was a calm, full,
late summer night, so rich and sweet it wouldn't do to
think too much about it. There were the low mountains
outside the city, covered with heavy late summer green,

and the long roads that went tilting through them, winding on forever.

"I don't want to hear about it any more," I said. "I don't want to talk about it. I've done the best I could." I told him about Yancey Clements.

"She's run up a blind alley and won't believe it," he said. "Can't you understand it? That minute she looked up and saw him watching, blank as a mirror, but as if a mirror could look back, admire, finally possess. . . ."

He had clenched his hand beside me in the dark and before I knew it, I had grasped it, trying to get the fingers open and relaxed. "I wish I'd never mentioned her," I said. "We always had such a good time till she got into everything. Why don't you just stop it?"

"Stop it?" He did unclench his hand, take mine and give it an affectionate squeeze, which went through me deep and clear. But it was only affection; that was all. "Stop it how? How?"

She was almost present then, his thought of her had summoned her before us both, alive in the strong disaster of her looks, which his intelligence and wit and everything I admired about him could only multiply until she had wrapped him up in a million ways and drawn him endlessly down. She, too, he was saying, with fine logic, had fallen for herself; it was not Yancey Clements she wanted, only that the lightning stroke of his look had thrown her off balance, maybe for good and all.

"If you don't stop it," I said, "it's just going to go on down forever, like the bottomless pit. Isn't it?"

At long last, he agreed. "You're right. I'm going to let it go." He got up and walked away, vanished into the night among the thick tree shadows. I wanted to run after him, had wanted to maybe for months now, but all this of Judith had trapped and denied my own feelings for him. They rose now, swept over me and fell; my heart ran after him, but I never moved at all. The words I might have said had all been taken.

He came to the house the next afternoon. I was upstairs working so did not see him on the street, and he must have just walked in without knocking, because no one challenged him or went to the door. I heard his first step down below and knew what had happened. The whole house knew it too, that ramified abode of women, women, women, over the long years. Turret to basement, it had needed this for a long time, that stride in the hall, that step on the stairs. Out in the upstairs corridor, I heard him blundering, trying one door after another, saying "Judith? Judith?" Then he found her. "Who?" she said, and then with a low cry, filled with surprise, opening toward joy, "Scott? Oh, Scott!" She must have risen then, out of her ruins, to go to him. I heard her stumble, fall and get up, or be lifted up by him.

Judith came to my room after he left. It was just at twilight. The spell was broken; as if to prove it, there had even been some rain. She had emerged at last, with new purpose, to bathe and dress, had put up her hair, got make-up on, stained her shoes fresh as chalk, and slipped into the lime-green dress, which hung on her limbs like a nightdress or a robe.

"You did it," she said, reflectively. "It was all because

you talked to him, wasn't it? But one thing," she continued, leaning in the doorway. "One thing. You've got to understand it. I didn't know you knew him."

"It's a lie," I said. "A lie! You must have known, you had to know! You not only knew, you used what you knew, every bit. You used me to make him come back. You can't deny it!"

She shook her lovely head; it was gaunt and rapacious now as some tall white bird, one with a great latent wing-spread for long flight. Where would she lead him to, where would she drop him when she moved furiously on to some other high perch, to astonish and confound whoever found her there? My heart filled up with dread. For him, I guess; that was where the dread started, but it had a way of spreading: it was more than just for him.

"Don't look at me like that," she said, raising her hand uneasily to touch her hair. "Why are you looking that way?"

"How could he do it, come here, come to you, when he knows about Yancey Clements? You were ready to crawl to that awful boy, that peeper, that vile, stupid, no-account . . ." I couldn't go on. But the questions forced themselves up anyway, kept rising to my lips. "Are they so much alike to you, you can't tell the difference? How could you want them both? How could you?"

Her head had snapped back, and her features strained to the force of my innocent words, as though I were striking her. I saw this, and stopped. In the silence (in which she could have turned and walked away but did not), I saw suddenly appear before my eyes identical streaks of tears from the corners of her eyes downward.

"I don't know," she whispered at last. "Oh, believe me, I don't know why."

I turned back to my work table, on which papers and books had been scrambled about and ink spilled, a great mess. "It's his most important time," I said. "Right at the end. Exams and all."

"You cared for him, didn't you?"

"Yes, but I . . ." I nodded, and with a strong releasing sigh that shook me, confessed it. "Yes."

She melted from the threshold, vanished. She had taken that from me, too, I realized, had come for it and easily taken it, my one privacy. She had had to have it, and so had demanded it.

She went out shortly after, going toward whatever place he had said; bone-thin and swift, moving—inexorable, indifferent, and sublime—toward him, as he desired. I watched through the window till I could no longer see her, and only the empty street was there, lit by street-lights.

The White Azalea

Two letters had arrived for Miss Theresa Stubblefield: she put them in her bag. She would not stop to read them in American Express, as many were doing, sitting on benches or leaning against the walls, but pushed her way out into the street. This was her first day in Rome and it was June.

An enormous sky of the most delicate blue arched overhead. In her mind's eye—her imagination responding fully, almost exhaustingly, to these shores' peculiar powers of stimulation—she saw the city as from above, telescoped on its great bare plains that the ruins marked, aqueducts and tombs, here a cypress, there a pine, and all round the low blue hills. Pictures in old Latin books returned to her: the Appian Way Today, the Colosseum, the Arch of Constantine. She would see them, looking just as they had in the books, and this would make up a part of her delight. Moreover, nursing various Stubblefields—her aunt, then her mother, then her father—through their lengthy illnesses (everybody could tell you the Stubblefields were always sick), Theresa had had a chance to read quite a lot. England, France, Germany, Switzerland, and Italy had all been rendered for her time and again, and between the prescribed hours of pills and tonics, she had conceived a dreamy passion by lamplight, to see all these places with her own eyes. The very night after her father's funeral she had thought, though never admitted to a soul: *Now I can go. There's nothing to stop me now.* So here it was, here was Italy, anyway, and terribly noisy.

In the street the traffic was really frightening. Cars, taxis, buses, and motorscooters all went plunging at once down the narrow length of it or swerving perilously around a fountain. Shoals of tourists went by her in national groups —English school girls in blue uniforms, German boys with cameras attached, smartly dressed Americans looking in shop windows. Glad to be alone. Theresa climbed the splendid outdoor staircase that opened to her left. The Spanish Steps.

Something special was going on here just now—the annual display of azalea plants. She had heard about it the night before at her hotel. It was not yet complete: work-men were unloading the potted plants from a truck and placing them in banked rows on the steps above. The aza-leas were as large as shrubs, and their myriad blooms, many still tight in the bud, ranged in color from purple through fuchsia and rose to the palest pink, along with many white ones too. Marvellous, thought Theresa, climbing in her portly, well-bred way, for she was someone who had learned that if you only move slowly enough you have time to notice everything. In Rome, all over Europe, she intended to move very slowly indeed.

Halfway up the staircase she stopped and sat down. Other people were doing it, too, sitting all along the wide banisters and leaning over the parapets above, watching

the azaleas mass, or just enjoying the sun. Theresa sat with
her letters in her lap, breathing Mediterranean air. The sun
warmed her, as it seemed to be warming everything, perhaps even the underside of stones or the chill insides of
churches. She loosened her tweed jacket and smoked a cigarette. Content . . . excited; how could you be both at
once? Strange, but she was. Presently, she picked up the
first of the letters.

A few moments later her hands were trembling and her
brow had contracted with anxiety and dismay. *Of course,
one of them would have to go and do this! Poor Cousin
Elec*, she thought, tears rising to sting in the sun, *but why
couldn't he have arranged to live through the summer?
And how on earth did I ever get this letter anyway?*

She had reason indeed to wonder how the letter had
managed to find her. Her Cousin Emma Carraway had
written it, in her loose high old lady's script—t's carefully
crossed, but l's inclined to wobble like an old car on the
downward slope. Cousin Emma had simply put Miss Theresa Stubblefield, Rome, Italy, on the envelope, had
walked up to the post office in Tuxapoka, Alabama, and
mailed it with as much confidence as if it had been a birthday card to her next-door neighbor. No return address
whatsoever. Somebody had scrawled American Express,
Piazza di Spagna?, across the envelope, and now Theresa
had it, all as easily as if she had been the President of the
Republic or the Pope. Inside were all the things they
thought she ought to know concerning the last illness,
death, and burial of Cousin Alexander Carraway.

Cousin Emma and Cousin Elec, brother and sister—un-
married, devoted, aging—had lived next door to the Stub-

blefields in Tuxapoka from time immemorial until the Stubblefields had moved to Montgomery fifteen years ago. Two days before he was taken sick, Cousin Elec was out worrying about what too much rain might do to his sweetpeas, and Cousin Elec had always preserved in the top drawer of his secretary a mother-of-pearl paper knife which Theresa had coveted as a child and which he had promised she could have when he died. *I'm supposed to care as much now as then, as much here as there*, she realized, with a sigh. *This letter would have got to me if she hadn't even put Rome, Italy, on it.*

She refolded the letter, replaced it in its envelope, and turned with relief to one from her brother George.

But alack, George, when *he* had written, had only just returned from going to Tuxapoka to Cousin Elec's funeral. He was full of heavy family reminiscence. All the fine old stock was dying out, look at the world today. His own children had suffered from the weakening of those values which he and Theresa had always taken for granted, and as for his grandchildren (he had one so far, still in diapers), he shuddered to think that the true meaning of character might never dawn on them at all. A life of gentility and principle such as Cousin Elec had lived had to be known at first hand. . . .

Poor George! The only boy, the family darling. Together with her mother, both of them tense with worry lest things should somehow go wrong, Theresa had seen him through the right college, into the right fraternity, and though pursued by various girls and various mammas of girls, safely married to the right sort, however much in the early years of that match his wife, Anne, had not seemed to understand poor George. Could it just be, Theresa wondered, that Anne had understood only too well, and that George all along was extraordinary only in the degree to which he was dull?

As for Cousin Alexander Carraway, the only thing Theresa could remember at the moment about him (except his paper knife) was that he had had exceptionally long hands and feet and one night about one o'clock in the morning the whole Stubblefield family had been aroused to go next door at Cousin Emma's call—first Papa, then Mother, then Theresa and George. There they all did their uttermost to help Cousin Elec get a cramp out of his foot. He had hobbled downstairs into the parlor, in his agony, and was sitting, wrapped in his bathrobe, on a footstool. He held his long clenched foot in both hands, and this and his contorted face—he was trying heroically not to cry out—made him look like a large skinny old monkey. They all surrounded him, the family circle, Theresa and George as solemn as if they were watching the cat have kittens, and Cousin Emma running back and forth with a kettle of hot water which she poured steaming into a white enamelled pan. "Can you think of anything to do?" she kept repeating. "I hate to call the doctor but if this keeps up I'll just have to! Can you think of anything to do?" "You might treat it like the hiccups," said Papa. "Drop a cold key down his back." "I just hope this happens to you someday," said Cousin Elec, who was not at his best. "Poor Cousin Elec," George said. He was younger than Theresa: she remembered looking down and seeing his great round eyes, while at the same time she was dimly aware that her mother and father were not unamused. "Poor Cousin Elec."

Now, here they both were, still the same, George full of round-eyed woe, and Cousin Emma in despair. Theresa shifted to a new page.

"Of course (George's letter continued), there are practical problems to be considered. Cousin Emma is alone in that big old house and won't hear to parting from it. Robbie and Beryl tried their best to persuade her to come and stay with them, and Anne and I have told her she's more than welcome here, but I think she feels that she might be an imposition, especially as long as our Rosie is still in high school. The other possibility is to make arrangements for her to let out one or two of the rooms to some teacher of good family or one of those solitary old ladies that Tuxapoka is populated with—Miss Edna Whittaker, for example. But there is more in this than meets the eye. A new bathroom would certainly have to be put in. The wallpaper in the back bedroom is literally crumbling off. . . ." (Theresa skipped a page of details about the house.) "I hope if you have any ideas along these lines you will write me about them. I may settle on some makeshift arrangements for the summer and wait until you return in the fall so we can work out together the best. . . ."

I really shouldn't have smoked a cigarette so early in the day, thought Theresa, it always makes me sick. I'll start sneezing in a minute, sitting on these cold steps. She got up, standing uncertainly for a moment, then moving aside to let go past her, talking, a group of young men. They wore shoes with pointed toes, odd to American eyes, and narrow trousers, and their hair looked unnaturally black and slick. Yet here they were obviously thought to be handsome, and felt themselves to be so. Just then a man approached her with a tray of cheap cameos, Parker fountain pens, rosaries, papal portraits. "No," said Theresa. "No, no!" she said. The man did not wish to leave. He knew how to spread himself against the borders of the space that had to separate them. Carrozza rides in the park, the Colosseum by moonlight, he specialized. . . . Theresa turned away to escape, and climbed to a higher landing where the steps divided in two. There she walked to the far left and leaned on a vacant section of banister, while the vendor picked himself another well-dressed American lady, carrying a camera and a handsome alligator bag, ascending the steps alone. Was he ever successful, Theresa wondered. The lady with the alligator bag registered interest, doubt, then indignation; at last, alarm. She cast about as though looking for a policeman: this really shouldn't be allowed! Finally, she scurried away up the steps.

Theresa Stubblefield, still holding the family letters in one hand, realized that her whole trip to Europe was viewed in family circles as an interlude between Cousin Elec's death and "doing something" about Cousin Emma. They were even, Anne and George, probably thinking themselves very considerate in not hinting that she really should cut out "one or two countries" and come home in August to get Cousin Emma's house ready before the teachers came to Tuxapoka in September. Of course, it wasn't Anne and George's fault that one family crisis seemed to follow another, and weren't they always em-

phasizing that they really didn't know what they would
do without Theresa? *The trouble is,* Theresa thought, *that
while everything that happens there is supposed to matter
supremely, nothing here is supposed even to exist. They
would not care if all of Europe were to sink into the ocean
tomorrow. It never registered with them that I had time to
read all of Balzac, Dickens, and Stendhal while Papa was
dying, not to mention everything in the city library after
Mother's operation. It would have been exactly the same
to them if I had read through all twenty-six volumes of
Elsie Dinsmore.*

She arranged the letters carefully, one on top of the
other. Then, with a motion so suddenly violent that she
amazed herself, she tore them in two.

"*Signora?*"

She became aware that two Italian workmen, carrying a
large azalea pot, were standing before her and wanted her
to move so that they could begin arranging a new row of
the display.

"*Mi diapiace, signora, ma . . . insomma. . . .*"

"Oh . . . put it there!" She indicated a spot a little distance away. They did not understand. "*Ponere . . . la.*"
A little Latin, a little French. How one got along! The
workmen exchanged a glance, a shrug. Then they obeyed
her. "*Va bene, signora.*" They laughed as they returned
down the steps in the sun.

Theresa was still holding the torn letters, half in either
hand, and the flush was fading slowly from her brow.
What a strong feeling had shaken her! She observed the
irregular edges of paper, so crudely wrenched apart, and
began to feel guilty. The Stubblefields, it was true, were

proud and prominent, but how thin, how vulnerable was that pride it was so easy to prove, and how local was that prominence there was really no need to tell even them. But none could ever deny that the Stubblefields meant well; no one had ever challenged that the Stubblefields were good. Now out of their very letters, their sorrowful eyes, full of gentility and principle, appeared to be regarding Theresa, one of their own who had turned against them, and soft voices, so ready to forgive all, seemed to be saying, "Oh, Theresa, how *could* you?"

Wasn't that exactly what they had said when, as a girl, she had fallen in love with Charlie Wharton, whose father had unfortunately been in the pen? Ever so softly, ever so distressed: "Oh, Theresa, how *could* you?" Never mind. That was long ago, over and done with, and right now something clearly had to be done about these letters.

Theresa moved forward, and leaning down she dropped the torn sheets into the azalea pot which the workmen had just left. But the matter was not so easily settled. What if the letters should blow away? One could not bear the thought of that which was personal to the Stubblefields chancing out on the steps where everyone passed, or maybe even into the piazza below to be run over by a motorscooter, walked over by the common herd, spit upon, picked up and read, or—worst of all—returned to American Express by some conscientious tourist, where tomorrow, filthy, crumpled, bedraggled, but still legibly, faithfully relating Cousin Elec's death and Cousin Emma's grief, they might be produced to confront her.

Theresa moved a little closer to the azalea pot and sat down beside it. She covered the letters deftly, smoothing the earth above them and making sure that no trace of paper showed above ground. The corner of Cousin Emma's envelope caught on a root and had to be shoved under, a painful moment, as if a letter could feel anything—how absurd! Then Theresa realized, straightening up and rubbing dirt off her hand with a piece of Kleenex from her bag, that it was not the letters but the Stubblefields that she had torn apart and consigned to the earth. This was certainly the only explanation of why the whole curious sequence, now that it was complete, had made her feel so marvellously much better.

Well, I declare! Theresa thought, astonished at herself, and in that moment it was as though she stood before the statue of some heroic classical woman whose dagger dripped with stony blood. *My goodness!* she thought, drowning in those blank exalted eyeballs: *Me!*

So thrilled she could not, for a time, move on, she stood noting that this particular azalea was one of exceptional beauty. It was white, in outline as symmetrically developed as an oak tree, and blooming in every part with a ruffled, lacy purity. The azalea was, moreover, Theresa recalled, a Southern flower, one especially cultivated in Alabama. Why, the finest in the world were said to grow in Bellingrath Gardens near Mobile, though probably they had not heard about that in Rome.

Now Miss Theresa Stubblefield descended quickly, down, down, toward the swarming square, down toward the fountain and all the racket, into the Roman crowd. There she was lost at once in the swirl, nameless, anonymous, one more nice rich American tourist lady.

But she cast one last glance back to where the white

azalea stood, blooming among all the others. By now the stone of the great staircase was all but covered over. A group of young priests in scarlet cassocks went past, mounting with rapid, forward energy, weaving their way vividly aloft among the massed flowers. At the top of the steps the twin towers of a church rose, standing clearly outlined on the blue air. Some large white clouds, charged with pearly light, were passing overhead at a slow imperial pace.

Well, it certainly is beyond a doubt the most beautiful family funeral of them all! thought Theresa. *And if they should ever object to what I did to them,* she thought, recalling the stone giantess with her dagger and the gouts of blood hanging thick and gravid upon it, *they've only to read a little and learn that there have been those in my position who haven't acted in half so considerate a way.*

Wisteria

Charles Webley rather liked his hostess, though he imagined a lot of people didn't. She talked too much, for one thing, but then you didn't have to listen. Her voice was pleasing and made a soothing ripple of sound which broke in occasional laughter. At the moment she didn't mean to be taken seriously. She was hefty, to put it mildly, way too big by English standards. But, he thought, lazily tolerant, she was not overbearing, no Brünnhilde she, and one could always be reminded of the jolly Dutch women, in popular conception at least, with their butter-colored hair cut short and their rotund, softly elephantine, white limbs. But Evaline's hair, in the years since they had met, must have gone from blonde to grey, or why would she have got it stiffly done up in what she probably thought of as silver gilt, but which looked to him like new aluminum? How, charitably, was he to picture her in Dutch clogs and a peaked cap now that her waistline had vanished? She was at present all baled up in Roman silks. He gave a short explosive laugh.

"Thought you'd like that, Charles." She had just wound up a little story, no word of which had reached him.

He wandered out into the garden. The apartment was

on the ground floor, unusual in Rome, with a wisteria vine
thickly roofing the terrace. Blooms like bunches of pale
grapes hung down and grazed his tall head. One cluster, so
disturbed, suddenly shed all its blossoms upon him. Laven-
der flowers fell from his head to his shoulders and scattered on the paving about his feet; and one final petal, letting go like the rest, landed in his martini. He stood regarding it, trying to grasp, hold on to, the surprising moment, generous and fragrant, which had created a sharp
start in his breast, resembling love. He looked up for
someone to share it with.

"Do you prefer flowers to lemon peel?"

The woman—not young, not old, thin, rather sallow,
with large brown eyes, nondescript dark hair, a plain navy
dress—was not the right one for that moment, nor had she
said the right thing. She did not in any way amplify that
tender instant, the heart of it, when the wisteria petal had
actually touched the chill surface of the gin.

"I don't think that ever happened to me before," he
said.

"I never saw it happen to anybody before."

"At my age you have to be careful about saying what's
never happened. At your age you don't have to."

Her eyes acknowledged his compliment. "How long
have you known Evaline?"

Wrong again, he thought, but saw the reason: she was
shy, and knowing that, he had to answer, no matter how
much questions like this bored him.

"Ages. I knew her first husband; the only one, I mean.
We were in school together, kept crossing paths."

"What's he like?"

"Good sort. Pleasant." He got impatient. "Hell, what's anyone like?"

One of the doors opening out on the garden filled up to two-thirds of its height and all its breadth, as Evaline herself emerged upon them.

"So glad you met Dorothy, Charles. She paints, you know. Would never tell you, so how could you know? I've one of her things in the guest room. You've got to see it before you go."

"Indeed I must."

The girl averted her face. There was a kind of subdued distaste in it, an aversion to being patronized, he supposed. If the painting had been put in the salon, instead of stuck away out of sight. . . . As it was, why mention it at all? He experienced a sudden, genuine feeling for this girl after all. He could read her, as clear as anything. The maid was elsewhere, so Evaline herself was taking their glasses.

"So grand to see Charles again. Such a surprise when you rang. It really did give me a lift; you've no idea."

He agreed, and in a way really meant it. Whatever mix-ups and misunderstandings there had been in the past, back when she lived in London, why remember them now? Why give any importance, at this late date, to the ins and outs of it all? Old friends were best because they didn't matter so much any more; it was all coasting from now on out, and there was downright comfort in the thought.

"I was lucky to find you in. I think of you Romans' being always in motion, especially from May on. The mountains or the sea. Going off somewhere interesting."

"He's being absurd," Evaline explained to Dorothy. "No, if you must know, I'm here nearly all the time these days. You'll get out of me all the reasons why." She thus reminded him, as she turned away for the drinks, that he had invited her to dine with him that evening, so getting himself asked to one of her little cocktail gatherings beforehand. Evaline being charming and parcelled out at one of her own parties was one thing; Evaline as she would shortly be across a narrow table from him, pouring out her various troubles, complexes, illnesses, labyrinthine relationships, was another. He couldn't count on just happening to laugh when she finished being witty, just happening to cloud over when the theme was tragic; that would be pushing his luck. No, he would have to listen.

"Listen," he said urgently to the girl. The pace of the chatter had stepped up in the room behind. The knots of guests were now mainly standing, except for a jet-haired Roman girl settled in an armchair with men hovering about her on hassocks and smaller chairs. Soon they would finish this round and take a notion to disperse, gather up hats and purses, go scattering out into the open.

"Listen." He caught the girl by the elbow and steered her aside, out of the central area of the garden, back turned toward the company. He noticed how light she was and how maneuverable. Her head turned to him with a sort of serene attentiveness, and he remembered the quiet fall of the blossoms.

"Do you know Evaline well?" It was a similar question to her own, but she had been making conversation; he was not.

"I've known her off and on for years. Five in all, I guess." She added, "She's been very kind to me."

"Oh, stop it." He almost snapped. "What I mean is, do

you see her alone, and if so, does she confide in you? She must. She confides in everyone."

The girl nodded. "I've noticed that. A few times—yes, I would say she's been confidential." She risked something. "I don't like so much confidence."

"I know, I know. Italian lovers, money problems, quarrels, defections of friends . . ." Now he had got her with him, and she actually grinned. He continued, "Has she mentioned her husband?"

"Well, often—yes, I'd say very often, but always rather distantly. I long ago decided he must have been a myth."

"I'm having dinner with her, right after this, taking her out somewhere. Does she know? I keep asking myself. Does she know he's dead?"

"Good Lord, no! At least, I think not."

"Why?"

"Well, she'd have said. She'd have called up everybody, right away."

"I assumed she would have been told. But then he did marry again, and Rome is a long way off." He walked away with the girl at his elbow; they had really drifted now, apart from the gathering. "I came early to this party, for just that reason, to mention it, offer condolences, whatever people do. She never seemed aware of it. No opening of any kind. Yet it happened over a month ago, in London." He stared down at his feet in deep preoccupation, a business habit. "Well," he demanded of her, "what would you conclude?"

"I think that everybody must have thought that someone else had told her."

"Just as I have. Is that what you mean?"

"Yes. Just as you have."

They turned to find Evaline before them once more, their fresh drinks hospitably extended in either hand. "Here you are, you two." She was beaming upon them, but implicit in that smile was the knowledge that he was safely landed as her escort for the evening. The restaurant she would suggest was already selected. It would be nice to be seen with him. She could afford to pretend to Dorothy that, seeing the two of them alone out there, she had assumed a flirtation was in progress. Charles Webley and Dorothy dutifully took their glasses.

The predictable moment arrived. The guests were flowing out to say their goodbyes, remarking on the wisteria, a choice conversation piece, and Evaline, full of a loving glow on its behalf, told the history of how it had been planted there, what narrow escapes it had had, what she had done to make it flourish and flower.

"They bloom twice, you know. Oh, yes, indeed. Early, and late."

She saw she had gained the center of the party and was holding it. To make the most of it, she nudged the last phrase into a double meaning, as though it referred to women, to all women, herself especially. She then touched her hand to the gathered silks above her heart.

The party caught the idea and laughed gaily, as she had meant them to, and Charles Webley and the girl Dorothy involuntarily struck glances. All was said, framed and frozen, in that instant's communication, and as one they turned off in opposite ways.

The Visit

The children were playing through the long empty rooms
of the villa, shuttered now against the sunlight during the
hottest hour of the day. The great man had gone to take a
nap.

Before she had come to Italy, Judy thought that siesta
was the word all Latins used for a rest after lunch, but she
had learned that you said this only in Spain. In Italy you
went to *riposarsi*, and this was exactly what the great man
had done.

It was unfortunate because Bill had built up so to this
visit. To be invited to see Thompson was, for almost anyone in the academic world, the token of something superior; but in Bill's particular field, it was the treasure, the X
mark on the ancient map.

Judy often thought that Bill had an "and-then" sort of
career. Graduate courses, a master's degree. A dissertation,
a doctorate. A teaching appointment, scholarly articles.
And then, and then. Promotion, the dissertation published,
and clearly ahead on the upward road they could discern
the next goal: a second, solidly important, possibly even
definitive book. A grant from the Foundation was a natu-

ral forward step, and Bill then got to take his wife to Italy for a year. In Italy, as all knew, was Thompson.

Bill and Judy Owens had arrived in October; now it was June. All year Bill had worked on his book, the ambitious one, all about ancient Roman portraiture; Judy had typed for him, and manuscript had piled up thickly. They went about looking at museums, at ancient ruins and new excavations. They met other attractive young American couples who were abroad on fellowships and scholarships, studied Italian, attended lectures, and fequently complained about not getting to know more of the natives.

But all the time Bill and Judy did not mistake what the real thread was, nor which and-then they were working on now. The book would get written somehow; but what prestige it would gain for Bill if only he had the right to make a personal reference to Thompson even once—and more than once would be overdoing it. Should it go in the introduction, or the preface, or the acknowledgements, or the text itself? This would depend on the nature of what Thompson, at last, yielded; and did it matter so much where the single drop of essence landed, when it would go to work for one anywhere, regardless?

Bill was always thorough—he was anything but aimless; but in this matter he became something he had never been before: he grew crafty as hell. He plotted the right people to write and the best month for them to receive a letter. He considered the number of paragraphs which should go by before Thompson was even mentioned. In some cases Thompson's name was not even allowed to appear; yet his presence (such was Bill's skill) would breathe from every word. Pressure could be brought to bear in some cases:

Bill had not been in the academic world fifteen years for nothing; and everything in American life is, in the long run, as we all know, competitive. He poked fun at his scheming mind—yet the goal was important to him, and he pressed forward in an innocent, bloodthirsty way, as if it were a game he had to win.

At last, in May, just when it seemed that nothing would happen, a letter arrived from a Professor Eakins, Bill's mentor in graduate school. "By the way," Eakins wrote (after a certain number of paragraphs had gone by), "I had a letter from Thompson recently saying that if any one of my students would be in the neighborhood of Genoa during June, he would be most welcome at the villa. I could think of no one I would rather have call on him than you, Bill. Of course, if you are planning to be in Sicily at that time, you'll let me know, so that—"

But Bill was not planning to be anywhere near Sicily in June.

From Genoa, in June, Bill and Judy had gone straight to the village in the mountains nearest to Thompson's villa. This village was the usual take-off point for people who went to see Thompson. Judy had pointed out that another village nearby had, according to the guide book, a more interesting church, with a cosmatesque cloister and a work in the baptistry attributed by some to Donatello (Judy loved Donatello), but Bill decided that this was no time for anything unorthodox. So they went to the usual village.

All kinds of legends were attached to the place. Some people had waited there for a week or more in the only halfway decent *pensione*, had dispatched all the proper credentials to the villa, but had never received any word at all. They had finally had to leave, looking out of the rear window of the taxi all the way to the station, until the mountain shut out the village forever. But no one could ever be personally encountered to whom anything of the sort had happened, and Bill had decided that it was only a Kafka-like nightmare which had accrued of itself to the Thompson image—he put it out of his mind by force.

He refused to recall it, even after he and Judy had sat waiting in the village for two days. He read the books he had brought to read, and Judy typed the chapter she had brought to type; then they proofread it together. They went out in the evenings and ate outdoors before a little restaurant under a string of colored lights. Here Judy, who got on rather well in Italian, answered all the waiter's questions about their son Henry, who had nine years and was now in care of his aunt in the *Stati Uniti*. The waiter said that she was much too young to have a nine-year-old son, and that her husband was a great scholar—one could see it *subito*. Judy enjoyed herself and drank up most of the wine. Light lingered in the mountains. They walked around and looked down at the view, an aspect of a splendid, darkening valley.

Bill threw himself down on a bench. Perhaps, he reflected aloud, Eakins was the wrong one to recommend him to Thompson. Who, after all, valued Eakins' work as highly as Eakins did? Eakins' large, fleshy, cultivated face all but materialized, with the thin, iron-grey hair and the thin waxed mustaches. It could be that Thompson thought so little of Eakins that any letter from or about Eakins could easily be tossed aside.

As he sat torturing himself this way, Judy leaned her elbows on the rough wall, looking far down at some twinkling lights. She said that if only they were religious instead of scholastic they would have come off better, since anyone at all could get an audience with the Pope. In fact, the problem seemed to be how to get out of one. In Rome, you might just pull a thread by accident and wind up buying a black veil and checking to see if you had the right gloves and shoes.

Bill said that scholastic was not the right word; it particularly connoted the Middle Ages. As Judy had finished only two years of college, Bill often had to put her right about things.

On their return to the *pensione*, the maid ran out and handed them a letter. "*È arrivata*," she said. It was somewhat embarrassing to be clearly seen through. Nonetheless, Bill's hour had struck. He and Judy were invited to lunch with Thompson on the following day.

Instead of driving their own car up to the villa, they took a taxi, as the proprietor of the *pensione* advised. He said that the way was extremely steep and dangerous. There were falling rocks, sharp curves, few markers. Their tires might be cut to pieces on the stones. Their water might boil away out of the radiator. They might lose the way entirely.

"How symbolic can you get?" Bill remarked. "Besides, his brother probably owns the taxi."

But all the proprietor said proved to be literally true. Bill and Judy were flung against each other several times on the curves. As the road threaded higher and higher, they dared not look out of the windows.

"I have to keep reminding myself," said Bill, shuddering away from a frightful declivity, "that this road may be leading me to the Thrace mosaics."

Judy knew about those mosaics, all from having typed so many letters. She knew as much as anybody. How they had been whatever the polite word was for smuggled out of the Middle East; how large the sums were that had gone for them, some over tables and some under; how museums and authorities of every nation could agree on no one but Thompson to receive them. Now they were at the villa. Some visitors had been allowed to peep at them, some even to have a brief try, as with a jigsaw puzzle, at matching this to that—a foot here, an arm there, and what prestige when the thing was talked about afterwards!

"If only you could see them, " Judy said.

"I can't think of any reason why I shouldn't," Bill said. The road had stabilized somewhat and he spoke with greater confidence, leaning back and crossing his legs. Judy smoothed her hair and agreed with him, then they were there.

The road flattened; a green plateau appeared before them, and set in it, at a fair distance, the villa. It looked like a photograph of itself. The tawny, bare façade was facing directly toward them. A colonnade ran out toward the left like a strong arm; it broke and softened the long savage drop of the mountain behind and framed in a half-embrace the grassy courtyard. There in the background, a hundred yards or so behind the villa, hung the ruin, the old castle. Rough and craggy, it was unused except artistically, as a backdrop, or to show people through (some visitors had reported being shown through), or perhaps for children to play in. Thompson's daughter, whose husband, the Prince of Gaeta, owned the villa, was said to have two children, and as if to prove that this was so, they at once appeared, a boy and girl, dressed in identical loose grey pinafores and long black stockings. They came out from among the shadows of the colonnade.

The radiator cap on the taxi had been removed for the journey, and Bill and Judy now chugged at a decorous pace into the courtyard, trailing a long plume of smoke. A dark man wearing English flannels came out of the villa and hastened to the colonnade, taking from behind a pillar a large green watering can. He poured water into the radiator of the taxi, then the cab driver handed him the radiator cap through the window, and he screwed it in place. "*È il principe,*" said the driver, over his shoulder. The prince himself!

"*Buon giorno,*" said the prince to the driver, sticking his head through the window.

"*Buon giorno, signor principe,*" returned the driver. "*Notizie?*"

Judy knew enough to follow that the prince was asking what was new and the driver was saying that nothing much was going on. Then the driver gave the prince a package of letters tied with a string.

The prince greeted his guests in English, opening the car door for them. The children had joined him and were standing nearby, side by side, looking at the newcomers with dark eyes, brilliant in their pale, inquisitive faces.

"Perhaps," said the prince, "you'd like to see our position before going inside?" He led the way across the courtyard to the right, where they saw the land drop completely away. Portions of a road, perhaps their own, could be seen arranged in broken bits along the sheer slopes, and far below, between boulders, they saw the silent blue and white curling of the sea.

They were received in a small sitting room furnished with much-sat-in overstuffed furniture and opening out on a large terrace. The prince had them sit down and the two children, having been already formally presented in the courtyard, tucked themselves away on stools. Though they did not stare, they certainly watched: two more, they were clearly saying to themselves, had arrived.

Flashing dark, affable smiles, the prince said that he sometimes rode back down to the village with the taxi driver but that it must be hot below. Judy and Bill agreed: the nights were cool but at midday especially it was indeed hot below. Presently Madame Thompson came in—one said "Madame" instead of "Mrs." or "Signora" possibly to give her the continental flavor she deserved, though she was not French but German, and Thompson was American. Her long straight grey hair was screwed into a knot at the back. She was wrapped in a coarse white shawl. They should all move out to the terrace, she suggested, because the view was vunderful. They moved out to the terrace and soon two young women came in. The one with the tray of aperitifs was a servant; the other, the one wearing bracelets and smoking a cigarette, was Thompson's daughter, the princess.

From the opposite end of the terrace, making all turn, Thompson himself strode in.

He was grizzly and vigorous, with heavy brown hands. He wore a cardigan, crumpled trousers that looked about to fall down, and carpet slippers. He advanced to the center of the group and halted, squinting in the strong sun.

Judy dared not look at Bill. She had seen him at many other rungs of the ladder, looking both fearful and hopeful, both nervous and brave, in desperate proportions only Bill could concoct, and her heart had gone out to him. But now, as he confronted the Great Man at last, she looked elsewhere. She knew that he was transferring his glass to his left hand; she knew that his grasp would be damp, shaky, and cold.

Almost as much as for Bill, however, Judy was anxious for herself. Why, she now wondered, had she thought it necessary to look so well? Bill, in carefully pressed flannels, with crisp greying hair and heavy glasses, looked as American as naturally as a Chinaman looked Chinese, but with her the thing had taken some doing, and, inspired by the idea of helping him, she had worked at it hard. Brushes and bottles and God knows what had got into it and what with her best costume, a cream-colored linen sheath with loose matching jacket, a strand of pearls, gold earrings, and shimmering brown hair, she looked ready to be mounted in an enlargement on a handsome page; but what had that to do with scholarship? The princess and her mother, Judy felt certain, did not own one lipstick between them. They dressed like peasants, forgetting the whole thing.

It's only that I know how little I know to talk about,

Judy thought. That's why I was so careful. What if they found out about all those books I haven't read? She shook hands with Thompson, but didn't say anything: she only smiled.

Bill, who used to be good at tennis—he and Judy had met one summer on a tennis court—found a means of cutting off the small talk with an opening question like a serve, something about a recent comparison of Byzantine and Roman portraiture. A moment later he was trotting off at Thompson's side, off toward the library, while words like monograph and research grant, Harvard and Cambridge, frothed about in their wake.

Judy was left alone with the family.

She asked them about their daily routine. The princess said she went down each afternoon to bathe in the sea. "But how do you get down?" Judy wanted to know. "Oh, by a stairway in back of the castle. It's quite a walk, but good for my figure." "Then do you walk back up?" "Oh, no. There's a ski lift a half-mile from the beach. It lands me on a plateau, a sort of meadow. Beautiful. You've no idea. In the spring it is covered with flowers. I love it. Then I walk back through the castle and home."

"So there's skiing here, too?" she asked the prince.

"Oh, no!" said the prince.

"He brought an old ski lift home from the Dolomites," the princess explained. "Just so I could ride up from the beach."

"Do you have a farm here?" Judy asked.

"Oh, no!" said the prince.

"He did at one time," said the princess.

"At one time, I did, yes. Then I spent some years in England. In England they are all so kind to the animals. Oh, very kind. When I came back for the first time I saw how cruel our peasants were. Not that they meant to be cruel. Yet they were—they were cruel! I tried to change them. But they would not change. So at last I sold the animals and sent away all the peasants."

"That's one solution," Judy agreed.

"He vill never eat the meat," said Madame Thompson. She smiled, deeply, like the Mona Lisa. "Never!"

"Oh, yes, the impression was a strong one. Also I am interested in Moral Rearmament. In England now there are so many thinking in this way. Now I will never eat meat again. To me it is eating flesh. *Carne!*"

It was not surprising, then, that they had *pasta* for lunch, followed by an omelet. Thompson sat at the head of the table.

"You should go to Greece," Thompson said to Bill. "Don't you plan to?"

"Greece isn't my field," Bill explained. "And of course my fellowship—"

"Fields and fellowships," said Thompson and gulped down some wine. "Fellowships and fields."

Bill remarked with a wry smile that Thompson himself had had one or two grants. "Oh, live on 'em!" Thompson cried. "Absolutely live on 'em. You people keep coming up the mountain—coming up the mountain. We must make it all work. How else?" His eye roved savagely around until it lighted on Judy: she felt as if her clothes were cracking suddenly away at the seams. Still observing her, Thompson said to Bill, "I'll tell you a subject that ten years ago I wouldn't have given a second thought to—at

your age I would have derided it. The relation of art to
economics."

"Oh, Lord, no," said Bill at once. "Not after 'The Byzantine Aesthetic.' "

"Very odd," said Thompson; "I feel exactly the same
about one subject as the other." He sighed. "Well, don't
tell Eakins on me, will you?"

"He'd think I was joking," Bill said.

"That summer in Paris," Thompson said, "when we met
Eakins. When was that?" He addressed his wife. Madame
Thompson had said nothing, it seemed to Judy, since her
remark about the meat the prince would not eat; but now
she began with patient, devoted, humorless accuracy to
trace out what was wanted. Her voice rolled out in heav-
ily muffled phrases, like something amplified through
clouds.

"It vas in 1927, the summer Eugene, your secretary for
ten years, had died at Cologne of pneumonia on the last
day of February. You decided to bring three articles later
called 'Some Aspects of the Renaissance'—"

"God!" Bill breathed, showing that he recognized the
title.

"—to rewrite in Paris. After Eugene's death you
thought alvays of the sculptures in the Louvre."

Memory rushed into Thompson, a back-lashing wave.
The wine of that long ago summer seemed to be crisping
his tongue. "Oh, yes, and there was Eakins wanting all the
same books as I in the Bibliothèque Nationale. He carried a
sandwich in his brief case. Very poor. One meal a day.
Some *poule* or other was giving him that. No fellowships
then. Nothing but fields. Some very green." He gave a

short laugh. "I don't say he *read* the books, of course. That might be asking too much of Eakins."

The maid was putting the dessert around, a *crème cara-mel*. Thompson said he never ate dessert and went shuffling out in his carpet slippers. They all sat eating in silence. The princess said she would soon be going down for a swim if the Owens would care to join her. "I know I shouldn't so soon after eating, but the walk is good for me." She drew herself in smartly. Bill's refusal included the hint that he intended to have more of a talk with Thompson before the visit was over. "Oh, but he has gone to rest," they all said. "He must have his rest."

Bill looked concerned, and the prince promised to take him into the library, where Thompson would certainly come the moment he got up. Then the prince took Judy out to see his roses. The garden was in back of the castle ruins, in a sheltered area between the mountain and the ruined wall, opening out toward the south. The prince had gone to a great deal of trouble. Roses were especially hard to cultivate in Italy. But he had admired them so in England. His were ravishing—broad blooms of pink, white, red, and yellow. Here they could distinctly hear the sea.

In the pauses between his bits of information the prince looked inquiringly at Judy as if he was wondering if there was something else he could do for himself. His life so far would have been like the sweep of a windshield wiper. Of course, he was a prince; of course, he had a villa and a castle, with the daughter of a famous man for his wife and roses and two beautiful children, and Moral Rearmament and English flannels, and if the peasants did not understand, he sent them away. If that was not enough, he did not eat the meat. Was there something else?

Judy noticed this, but felt on short acquaintance she really had nothing to suggest. She stood wondering whether, since the peasants and the animals were gone, the roses too were financed by the foundations, but she decided this line of thought was ungracious.

The children appeared from nowhere. "Now they will take you round the castle, if you like," the prince kindly said. "It is mainly in shadow, so you won't grow tired. But mind you don't let them tempt you to climb. They love it, but they are like cats. Say, 'No, no, come down!' "

He turned away, toward nothing.

Clambering around the castle, Judy came on a sort of enclosure, sunlit and quiet. She could smell warm earth beneath the grass. The air was sweet and soft, what Italians called *dolce*. There were some beautiful old broken chunks of ruin lying scattered about. Judy sat down on some ruined steps and rested her chin in her palm. The children called to her out of a tower but she said, "No, no, come down," so they did. The sky was radiant and gentle. She could glimpse the children at intervals, running past empty window gaps, until at last they leaped down on the grass before her.

Suddenly from behind the children, at a notch in the wall, the princess rose up. She was climbing; though as they could not see her feet, she seemed to be rising like a planet. She was rubbing her wet hair with a towel, and the sense and movement of the sea was about her.

Stopping still, she addressed a volley of Italian to the children. It would have been hard to convince anyone that her father was from Minnesota. Judy made out *"Che hai?"* *"Cattivo, tu!"* and *"Dammelo!"* which meant, she reasoned, that the children had something they shouldn't have which now was to be given to their mother. Then, as they at first hung back with their fists stuffed in the pockets of their pinafores, but finally obeyed, going forward and reaching out toward the princess, Judy glimpsed handful after handful of flashing blue stones, the purest, most vibrant blue she had ever seen. The color seemed to prank about the air for a moment with the freakish skip of lightning.

"Was the ski lift working?" a voice cried. Thompson himself was striding out to find them among the ruins. The princess came down from the wall and sat down quickly on a large fallen cornice. She had taken the stones, like eggs, in her towel, and now she quickly concealed them in it as well.

"It was working but not very well. It goes very *piano*. It also runs at an *angolo*."

"We must send Giuseppe down to look at the motor," Thompson said. "How was the sea?"

"Strong, but right," said the princess.

Judy saw by her watch that it was nearly three. Bill must be going nuts in the library, she knew; and here was Thompson grasping her arm and hustling her along a narrow path. They entered the villa by a side door and were at once standing facing one another in a narrow room with the remains of old frescoes peeling from the walls, a Renaissance chest in the corner, and a cold swept fireplace.

Thompson placed a hand like a bear's paw beneath her

chin; his coarse thumb, raking down her cheek from temple to chin, all but left, she felt, a long scar. "Beauty," he remarked. His hand fell away and whatever she was expecting next did not occur.

"My husband," said Judy, "is waiting to see you. You know, don't you, that he is a terribly important scholar."

"So Eakins said . . . but then I've never especially liked Eakins, do you? He says these things for some purpose. It is rather like playing cards. Perhaps it's all true. How am I to know? I was never a scholar." He confided this last somewhat eagerly, as though it had been the reason for finding her, and having her believe it mattered to him, Judy could not think why. He leaned back against the chest and folded his long arms. "You think I have to go and talk to him?" he debated with her. "You think that is the important thing?"

"I don't know. Oh, I really don't know!" She burst out with this—undoubtedly, the wrong thing—quite unexpectedly, surprising herself.

"Ummm," said Thompson, thinking it over. His eyes—large, pale, old, and, she supposed, ugly—searched hers. Unreasonable pain filled her for a moment: she longed to comfort him, but before she could think of how to, he tilted her head to an angle that pleased him, kissed her brow and shambled off, though in truth he seemed to trail a length of broken chain.

She was left to lose her way alone.

Corridors, wrongly chosen, led her to a room, a door, a small courtyard, a stretch of gravel, a dry fountain. She walked halfway to the fountain and turned to look back at the façade, which like the other was sunburnt and bare. It was surmounted by a noble crest, slightly askew—the prince's, doubtless. I should have told Thompson, she thought, that the children had got into the mosaics, but suppose it wasn't true? How could you say such a thing and not make an idiot of yourself if you were wrong?

As she stood, her shadow lying faithfully beside her in the uncompromising sun, a door in the wing to her left swung open and two Hindus, splendidly dressed, the man in a tailored dark suit wearing a scarlet turban, the woman in a delicate spangled sari that prickled over the gravel, walked past the fountain, past Judy, and disappeared through a door in the façade. She had raised her hand to them, she had called, but they had not looked up.

Bill was disappointed to the point of despair by his visit, which had yielded him only a scant half-hour with Thompson and a dusty monograph, published in 1928. Even the subject matter—Greek vase painting—was not in Bill's field. Thompson had told him seriously that for a man of his age, he had a wonderful liver. If Eakins had lived in Europe as long as he (Thompson) had, his (Eakins') liver would look like a bloody sponge.

"He's an organized disappointment," Bill complained, "and not very well organized at that. He didn't want to talk to me because he can't compete any more. He's completely out of the swim."

"I liked him," said Judy. "I just loved him, in fact."

"Doubtless. He has a taste for pretty girls. You overdid it, dressing so well. Did he chase you through the upstairs ballroom? That's what it's used for nowadays."

The taxi having reappeared for them promptly at four,

they were now speeding down the mountain at a suicidal clip; they clung to straps beside the windows, where many a scholarly pair had clung before. Leaping rocks and whipping around curves, the cab clanged like a factory.

"The children had got into the mosaics," Judy shouted.

"What?" Bill yelled. And when she repeated it, "That can't be true," he answered.

"Did you see the Hindu couple?" she asked, as they sped through a silent green valley.

"No," said Bill. "And please don't describe them." He said that he had a headache and was getting sick. He wondered if they would return alive.

From the corner of her eye, Judy saw a huge boulder, dislodged by their wheels, float out into a white gorge with the leisure of a dream.

The Fishing Lake

She was crossing the edge of the field, along the ridge, walking with a longer, more assured step now; she knew just about where he was. She knew because she had seen the jeep parked just off the road, where it got too soggy to risk and too narrow to go through without a limb batting you between the eyes, and she stopped the car about a stone's throw back from there. Something told her all along he would be at the lake. She cleared the ridge, and there he was just below her, down at the pier, tying up the boat. He didn't look up. She eased herself sidewise down the wet, loamy bank that released the heavy smell of spring with every step, and she was within a few feet of him before he said, still not looking up, "There ought to be a better boat down here. I spent half the time bailing. There used to be another boat."

"I think that's the same one," she said. "It's just that things get run down so in a little while. I bet the Negroes come and use it; there's no way to keep them from it."

"It's got a lock on it."

"Well, you know, they may just sit in it to fish. Either that or let the children play in it."

He had found the mooring chain now; it grated through

the metal hook in the prow, and he snapped the lock shut and stepped out on the pier.

"Did you catch anything?"

He leaned down and pulled up a meagre string—two catfish, a perch, one tiny goggle-eye. "The lake needs draining and clearing the worst kind. All around the bend there's the worst kind of silt and slime. The stink is going to get worse." He paused. "Or maybe you'd say that I'm the stinker."

"I didn't say that. I didn't say anything about it."

He stood with his back to her, hands hooked on his thighs, like somebody in the backfield waiting for the kickoff, and his hair, still streaked with color—sunburnt, yellow and light brown—made him seem a much younger man than he would look whenever he decided to turn around. "I would tell you that I'm going to quit it," he said, "but you know and I know that that just ain't true. I ain't ever going to quit it."

"It wasn't so much getting drunk. . . . I just thought that coming home to visit Mama this way you might have put the brakes on a little bit."

"I intended to. I honestly did."

"And then, if you had to pick somebody out, why on earth did you pick out Eunice Lisles?"

"Who would you have approved of?" he asked. He looked off toward the sunset; it was delicate and pale above the tender, homemade line of her late uncle's fishing lake, which needed draining, had a leaking boat and a rickety pier.

"Well, nobody," she said. "What a damn-fool question.

I meant, by the cool, sober light of day, surely you can see that Eunice Lisles—"

"I didn't exactly pick her out," he said. "For all I know, she picked me out." He lit a cigarette, striking the kitchen match on the seat of his trousers. He began to transfer the tackle box, the roach box, the worm can, and the minnow bucket from the boat to the pier. He next took the pole out of the boat and began to wind off the tackle. "Where we made our big mistake is ever saying we'd go out. We came to Mississippi to see your mother, we should have stayed with your mother."

"Well, I mean if it gets to where we can't accept an invitation—"

"It hasn't got to where anything," he said irritably. "I'm exactly the same today as I was yesterday, or a year ago. I'm a day or a year older. I've got a hangover worse than usual. And I would appreciate never having to hear anything more about Eunice Lisles."

Her uncle had made a bench near the pier—a little added thought, so very like him. It was for the older ladies to sit on when they brought their grandchildren or nieces and nephews down to swim, and he had had a shelter built over it as well, to shade their heads from the sun, but that had been torn down, probably by Negroes using it for firewood. She remembered playing endlessly around the pier when one of her aunts or her grandfather or Uncle Albert himself brought her down there, and at twilight like this in the summer seeing the men with their Negro rowers come back, solemn and fast, almost processional,

heading home from around both bends in the lake, shout-
ing from boat to boat, "Whadyacatch? Hold up yo'
string! Lemme *see* 'em, man!" The men would have been
secret and quiet all afternoon, hidden in the rich, hot
thicket quiet of the brush and stumps, the Negroes pad-
dling softly, holding and backing and easing closer, with
hardly a ripple of the dark water. Then, at supper up at
Uncle Albert's, there would be the fish dipped in corn-
meal, spitting and frying in the iron skillets and spewing
out the rich-smelling smoke, and platter after platter of
them brought in to the table. You ate till you passed out in
those days, and there wasn't any drinking to amount to
anything—maybe somebody sneaking a swallow or two
off out in the yard. Her husband always told her she was
wrong about this, that she had been too young to know,
but she was there and he wasn't, she said, and ought at
least to know better than he did. What she really meant
was that her family and their friends and relatives had
been the finest people thereabouts, and were noted for
their generosity and fair, open dealings, and would never
dream of getting drunk all the time, in front of people. He
might at least have remembered that this was her home
town.

She sat down carefully now on what was left of the
bench her uncle had made. She opened her bag. "I
brought you something." It was a slug of her sister-in-
law's bourbon she had poured out into a medicine bottle,
sneaking as though it were a major theft, and adding a bit
of water to the whiskey bottle to bring the level up again,
nearly to where it was. She knew that all the family had

their opinions. In the house she had kept as quiet as death all day, and so had they. The feeling was that gossip was flying around everywhere, just past the front gate and the back gate, looping and swirling around them.

"That was nice of you. By God, it was." He began to move methodically, slowly, holding back, but his sense of relief gave him a surer touch, so the top of the tackle box came clanging down in a short time, and he came up beside her, taking the small bottle and unscrewing the top. "Ladies first." He offered it to her. She laughed; he could always make her laugh, even if she didn't want to. She shook her head, and the contents of the bottle simply evaporated down his throat. "That's better." He sat companionably beside her; they had to sit close together to get themselves both on the bench.

"I reckon you feel like you get to the end of your rope sometimes," he sympathized. "I think maybe you might."

She had too much of a hangover herself to want even to begin to go into detail about what she felt.

"I don't feel any different toward you," he went on. "In fact, every time you do something like today—go right through your family without batting an eye, steal their whiskey for me out from under their noses, and come down here to get your fussing done in private—I love you that much more. I downright admire you."

She said, after a time, "You know, I just remembered, coming down here up past the sandpit that Uncle dug out to sand the lake with so we could swim without stepping ankle-deep in mud, there was this thing that happened. . . . I did it; I was responsible for it. I used to go there in the afternoons to get a suntan when we used to come and stay with Uncle Albert. And back then they had this wild dog—they thought for a long time it was a cooter, or some even said a bear—but it turned out to be a wild dog, who used to kill calves. So one day I was lying there sunbathing and I looked up and there was the dog—that close to the house! It scared me half to death. I just froze. I went tight all over and would have screamed, but I couldn't. I remembered what they said about not getting nervous around animals because it only frightens them, so I didn't say anything and didn't move, I just watched. And after a while, just at the top of the hill where the earth had been busted open to get at the sand, the dog lay down and put its head on its paws—it must have been part bulldog—and watched me. I felt this peaceful feeling—extremely peaceful. It stayed there about an hour and then it went away and I went away. So I didn't mention it. I began to doubt if it had really seen me, because I heard somewhere that dogs' vision is not like humans', but I guessed it knew in its way that I was there. And the next time I went, it came again. I think this went on for about a week, and once I thought I would go close enough to pat its head. I had got so it was the last thing I'd ever be scared of, but when it had watched me climb to within just about from here to the end of the pier away from it, it drew back and got up and backed off. I kept on toward it, and it kept on drawing back and it looked at me—well, in a personal sort of way. It was a sort of dirty white, because of a thin white coat with markings underneath. It looked partly blue. It was the ugliest thing I ever saw.

"Then it killed some more calves, and they had got people out to find it, and more showed up when the word got round, bringing their guns and all, and there was almost a dance on account of it, just because so many people were around. A dollar-pitching, a watermelon-cutting—I don't know what all. I was only about fifteen, and I told on it."

"*Told* on it?"

"Yes, I said that if they would go down to the sandpit at a certain time they would see it come out of the woods to the top of the hill on the side away from the house. And they went out and killed it."

"That's all?"

"That's all."

"And that's the worst thing you ever did?"

"I didn't say that. I mean, I felt the worst about it afterwards."

"You might have thought how those poor calves felt."

"I thought of that. It's not the same thing. The link was me. I betrayed him."

"You worry about this all the time?" He was teasing, somewhat.

"I hadn't thought of it in ten or maybe even fifteen years, until today, coming along the ridge just now. You can still see the sandpit."

At that moment, the bench Uncle Albert had built to make those long-dead ladies comfortable collapsed. They had been too heavy to sit on it, certainly, and shouldn't have tried. As though somebody had reached out of nowhere and jerked a chair from under them, just for a joke, it spilled them both apart, out on the pier.

They began to laugh. "Come out here next year," he said, in his flat-talking Georgia way, "there ain't going to be one splinter hanging on to one nail. Even the bailing can's got a hole rusted in it."

She kept on laughing, for it was funny and awful and absolutely true, and there was nothing to do about it.

A Southern
Landscape

If you're like me and sometimes turn through the paper reading anything and everything because you're too lazy to get up and do what you ought to be doing, then you already know about my home town. There's a church there that has a gilded hand on the steeple, with the finger pointing to Heaven. The hand looks normal size, but it's really as big as a Ford car. At least, that's what they used to say in those little cartoon squares in the newspaper, full of sketches and exclamation points—"Strange As It Seems," "This Curious World," or Ripley's "Believe It or Not." Along with carnivorous tropical flowers, the Rosetta stone, and the cheerful information that the entire human race could be packed into a box a mile square and dumped into Grand Canyon, there it would be every so often, that old Presbyterian hand the size of a Ford car. It made me feel right in touch with the universe to see it in the paper—something it never did accomplish all by itself. I haven't seen anything about it recently, but then, Ford cars have got bigger, and, come to think of it, maybe they don't even print those cartoons any more. The name of the town, in case you're trying your best to remember and can't, is Port Claiborne, Mississippi. Not that I'm *from* there; I'm from *near* there.

Coming down the highway from Vicksburg, you come to Port Claiborne, and then to get to our house you turn off to the right on State Highway No. 202 and follow along the prettiest road. It's just about the way it always was—worn deep down like a tunnel and thick with shade in summer. In spring, it's so full of sweet heavy odors they make you drunk, you can't think of anything—you feel you will faint or go right out of yourself. In fall, there is the rustle of leaves under your tires and the smell of them, all sad and Indian-like. Then in the winter, there are only dust and bare limbs, and mud when it rains, and everything is like an old dirt-dauber's nest up in the corner. Well, any season, you go twisting along this tunnel for a mile or so, then the road breaks down into a flat open run toward a wooden bridge that spans a swampy creek bottom. Tall trees grow up out of the bottom—willow and cypress, gum and sycamore—and there is a jungle of brush and vines—kudzu, Jackson vine, Spanish moss, grapevine, Virginia creeper, and honeysuckle—looping, climbing, and festooning the trees, and harboring every sort of snake and varmint underneath. The wooden bridge clatters when you cross, and down far below you can see water, lying still, not a good step wide. One bank is grassy and the other is a slant of ribbed white sand.

Then you're going to have to stop and ask somebody. Just say, "Can you tell me where to turn to get to the Summerall place?" Everybody knows us. Not that we *are* anybody—I don't mean that. It's just that we've been there forever. When you find the right road, you go right on up through a little wood of oaks, then across a field, across a cattle gap, and you're there. The house is nothing special, just a one-gable affair with a bay window and a front porch—the kind they built back around fifty or sixty years ago. The shrubs around the porch and the privet hedge around the bay window were all grown up too high the last time I was there. They ought to be kept trimmed down. The yard is a nice flat one, not much for growing grass but wonderful for shooting marbles. There were always two or three marble holes out near the pecan trees where I used to play with the colored children.

Benjy Hamilton swore he twisted his ankle in one of those same marble holes once when he came to pick me up for something my senior year in high school. For all I know, they're still there, but Benjy was more than likely drunk and so would hardly have needed a marble hole for an excuse to fall down. Once, before we got the cattle gap, he couldn't open the gate, and fell on the barbed wire trying to cross the fence. I had to pick him out, thread at a time, he was so tangled up. Mama said, "What were you two doing out at the gate so long last night?" "Oh, nothing, just talking," I said. She thought for the longest time that Benjy Hamilton was the nicest boy that ever walked the earth. No matter how drunk he was, the presence of an innocent lady like Mama, who said *"Drinking?"* in the same tone of voice she would have said *"Murder?,"* would bring him around faster than any number of needle showers, massages, ice packs, prairie oysters, or quick dips in December off the northern bank of Lake Ontario. He would straighten up and smile and say, "You made any more peach pickle lately, Miss Sadie?" (He could even say "peach pickle.") And she'd say no, but that there was always some of the old for him whenever he wanted any. And he'd say that was just the sweetest thing he'd ever heard of, but she didn't know what she was promising—anything as good as her peach pickle ought to be guarded like gold. And she'd say, well, for most anybody else she'd think twice before she offered any. And he'd say, if only everybody was as sweet to him as she was. . . . And they'd go on together like that till you'd think that all creation had ground and wound itself down through the vistas of eternity to bring the two of them face to face for exchanging compliments over peach pickle. Then I would put my arm in his so it would look like he was helping me down the porch steps out of the reflexes of his gentlemanly upbringing, and off we'd go.

It didn't happen all the time, like I've made it sound. In fact, it was only a few times when I was in school that I went anywhere with Benjy Hamilton. Benjy isn't his name, either; it's Foster. I sometimes call him "Benjy" to myself, after a big overgrown thirty-three-year-old idiot in *The Sound and the Fury*, by William Faulkner. Not that Foster was so big or overgrown, or even thirty-three years old, back then; but he certainly did behave like an idiot.

I won this prize, see, for writing a paper on the siege of Vicksburg. It was for the United Daughters of the Confederacy's annual contest, and mine was judged the best in the state. So Foster Hamilton came all the way over to the schoolhouse and got me out of class—I felt terribly important—just to "interview" me. He had just graduated from the university and had a job on the paper in Port

Claiborne—that was before he started work for the *Times-Picayune*, in New Orleans. We went into an empty classroom and sat down.

He leaned over some blank sheets of coarse-grained paper and scribbled things down with a thick-leaded pencil. I was sitting in the next seat; it was a long bench divided by a number of writing arms, which was why they said that cheating was so prevalent in our school—you could just cheat without meaning to. They kept trying to raise the money for regular desks in every classroom, so as to improve morals. Anyway, I couldn't help seeing what he was writing down, so I said, " 'Marilee' is all one word, and with an 'i,' not a 'y.' 'Summerall' is spelled just like it sounds." "Are you a senior?" he asked. "Just a junior," I said. He wore horn-rimmed glasses; that was back before everybody wore them. I thought they looked unusual and very distinguished. Also, I had noticed his shoulders when he went over to let the window down. I thought they were distinguished, too, if a little bit bony. "What is your ambition?" he asked me. "I hope to go to college year after next," I said. "I intend to wait until my junior year in college to choose a career."

He kept looking down at his paper while he wrote, and when he finally looked up at me I was disappointed to see why he hadn't done it before. The reason was, he couldn't keep a straight face. It had happened before that people broke out laughing just when I was being my most earnest and sincere. It must have been what I said, because I don't think I *look* funny. I guess I don't look like much of any one thing. When I see myself in the mirror, no adjective springs right to mind, unless it's "average." I am medium height, I am average weight, I buy "natural"-colored face powder and "medium"-colored lipstick. But I must say for myself, before this goes too far, that every once in a great while I look Just Right. I've never found the combination for making this happen, and no amount of reading the makeup articles in the magazines they have at the beauty parlor will do any good. But sometimes it happens anyway, with no more than soap and water, powder, lipstick, and a damp hairbrush.

My interview took place in the spring, when we were practicing for the senior play every night. Though a junior, I was in it because they always got me, after the eighth grade, to take parts in things. Those of us that lived out in the country Mrs. Arrington would take back home in her car after rehearsal. One night, we went over from the school to get a Coca-Cola before the drugstore closed, and there was Foster Hamilton. He had done a real nice article—what Mama called a "writeup." It was when he was about to walk out that he noticed me and said, "Hey." I said "Hey" back, and since he just stood there, I said, "Thank you for the writeup in the paper."

"Oh, that's all right," he said, not really listening. He wasn't laughing this time. "Are you going home?" he said.

"We are after 'while," I said. "Mrs. Arrington takes us home in her car."

"Why don't you let me take you home?" he said. "It might—it might save Mrs. Arrington an extra trip."

"Well," I said, "I guess I could ask her."

So I went to Mrs. Arrington and said, "Mrs. Arrington,

Foster Hamilton said he would be glad to drive me home."
She hesitated so long that I put in, "He says it might save
you an extra trip." So finally she said, "Well, all right,
Marilee." She told Foster to drive carefully. I could tell
she was uneasy, but then, my family were known as real
good people, very strict, and of course she didn't want
them to feel she hadn't done the right thing.

That was the most wonderful night. I'll never forget it.
It was full of spring, all restlessness and sweet smells. It
was radiant, it was warm, it was serene. It was all the
things you want to call it, but no word would ever be the
right one, nor any ten words, either. When we got close
to our turnoff, after the bridge, I said, "The next road is
ours," but Foster drove right on past. I knew where he
was going. He was going to Windsor.

Windsor is this big colonial mansion built back before
the Civil War. It burned down during the eighteen-
nineties sometime, but there were still twenty-five or more
Corinthian columns, standing on a big open space of
ground that is a pasture now, with cows and mules and
calves grazing in it. The columns are enormously high and
you can see some of the iron-grillwork railing for the
second-story gallery clinging halfway up. Vines cling to
the fluted white plaster surfaces, and in some places the
plaster has crumbled away, showing the brick underneath.
Little trees grow up out of the tops of columns, and
chickens have their dust holes among the rubble. Just
down the fall of the ground beyond the ruin, there are
some Negro houses. A path goes down to them.

It is this ignorant way that the hand of Nature creeps
back over Windsor that makes me afraid. I'd rather

there'd be ghosts there, but there aren't. Just some old story about lost jewelry that every once in a while sends somebody poking around in all the trash. Still, it is magnificent, and people have compared it to the Parthenon and so on and so on, and even if it makes me feel this undertone of horror, I'm always ready to go and look at it again. When all of it was standing, back in the old days, it was higher even than the columns, and had a cupola, too. You could see the cupola from the river, they say, and the story went that Mark Twain used it to steer by. I've read that book since, *Life on the Mississippi*, and it seems he used everything else to steer by, too—crawfish mounds, old rowboats stuck in the mud, the tassels on somebody's corn patch, and every stump and stob from New Orleans to Cairo, Illinois. But it does kind of connect you up with something to know that Windsor was there, too, like seeing the Presbyterian hand in the newspaper. Some people would say at this point, "Small world," but it isn't a small world. It's an enormous world, bigger than you can imagine, but it's all connected up. What Nature does to Windsor it does to everything, including you and me—there's the horror.

But that night with Foster Hamilton, I wasn't thinking any such doleful thoughts, and though Windsor can be a pretty scary-looking sight by moonlight, it didn't scare me then. I could have got right out of the car, alone, and walked all around among the columns, and whatever I heard walking away through the weeds would not have scared me, either. We sat there, Foster and I, and never said a word. Then, after some time, he turned the car around and took the road back. Before we got to my house, though, he stopped the car by the roadside and kissed me. He held my face up to his, but outside that he didn't touch me. I had never been kissed in any deliberate and accomplished way before, and driving out to Windsor in that accidental way, the whole sweetness of the spring night, the innocence and mystery of the two of us, made me think how simple life was and how easy it was to step into happiness, like walking into your own rightful house.

This frame of mind persisted for two whole days— enough to make a nuisance of itself. I kept thinking that Foster Hamilton would come sooner or later and tell me that he loved me, and I couldn't sleep for thinking about him in various ways, and I had no appetite, and nobody could get me to answer them. I half expected him at play practice or to come to the schoolhouse, and I began to wish he would hurry up and get it over with, when, after play practice on the second night, I saw him uptown, on the corner, with this blonde.

Mrs. Arrington was driving us home, and he and the blonde were standing on the street corner, just about to get in his car. I never saw that blonde before or since, but she is printed eternally on my mind, and to this good day if I'd run into her across the counter from me in the ten-cent store, whichever one of us is selling lipstick to the other one, I'd know her for sure because I saw her for one half of a second in the street light in Port Claiborne with Foster Hamilton. She wasn't any ordinary blonde, either—dyed hair wasn't in it. I didn't know the term "feather-bed blonde" in those days, or I guess I would have thought it. As it was, I didn't really think anything, or say anything, either, but whatever had been galloping along inside me for two solid days and nights came to a screeching halt. Somebody in the car said, being real funny, "Foster Hamilton's got him another girl friend." I just laughed. "Sure has," I said. "Oh, Mari-leee!" they all said, teasing me. I laughed and laughed.

I asked Foster once, a long time later, "Why didn't you come back after that night you drove me out to Windsor?"

He shook his head. "We'd have been married in two weeks," he said. "It scared me half to death."

"Then it's a mercy you didn't," I said. "It scares *me* half to death right now."

Things had changed between us, you realize, between that kiss and that conversation. What happened was—at least, the main thing that happened was—Foster asked me the next year to go to the high-school senior dance with him, so I said all right.

I knew about Foster by then, and that his reputation was not of the best—that it was, in fact, about the worst our county had to offer. I knew he had an uncommon thirst and that on weekends he went helling about the countryside with a fellow that owned the local picture show and worked at a garage in the daytime. His name was A. P. Fortenberry, and he owned a new convertible in a sickening shade of bright maroon. The convertible was always dusty—though you could see A. P. in the garage every afternoon, during the slack hour, hosing it down on the wash rack—because he and Foster were out in it almost every night, harassing the countryside. They knew every bootlegger in a radius of forty miles. They knew girls that lived on the outskirts of towns and girls that didn't. I guess "uninhibited" was the word for A. P. Fortenberry, but whatever it was, I couldn't stand him. He called me into the garage one day—to have a word with me about Foster, he said—but when I got inside he backed me into the corner and started trying it on. "Funny little old girl," he kept saying. He rattled his words out real fast. "Funny little old girl." I slapped him as hard as I could, which was pretty hard, but that only seemed to stimulate him. I thought I'd never get away from him—I can't smell the inside of a garage to this good day without thinking about A. P. Fortenberry.

When Foster drove all the way out to see me one day soon after that—we didn't have a telephone in those days—I thought he'd come to apologize for A. P., and I'm not sure yet he didn't intend for me to understand that without saying anything about it. He certainly put himself out. He sat down and swapped a lot of Port Claiborne talk with Mama—just pleased her to death—and then he went out back with Daddy and looked at the chickens and the peach trees. He even had an opinion on growing peaches, though I reckon he'd given more thought to peach brandy than he'd ever given to orchards. He said when we were walking out to his car that he'd like to take me to the senior dance, so I said O.K. I was pleased; I had to admit it.

Even knowing everything I knew by then (I didn't tell Mama and Daddy), there was something kind of glamorous about Foster Hamilton. He came of a real good family, known for being aristocratic and smart; he had uncles who were college professors and big lawyers and doctors and things. His father had died when he was a babe in arms (tragedy), and he had perfect manners. He had perfect manners, that is, when he was sober, and it was not that he departed from them in any intentional way when he was drunk. Still, you couldn't exactly blame me for being disgusted when, after ten minutes of the dance, I discovered that his face was slightly green around the temples and that whereas he could dance fairly well, he could not stand up by himself at all. He teetered like a baby that has caught on to what walking is, and knows that now is the time to do it, but hasn't had quite enough practice.

"Foster," I whispered, "have you been drinking?"

"Been *drinking?*" he repeated. He looked at me with a sort of wonder, like the national president of the W.C.T.U. might if asked the same question. "It's so close in here," he complained.

It really wasn't that close yet, but it was going to be. The gym doors were open, so that people could walk outside in the night air whenever they wanted to. "Let's go outside," I said. Well, in my many anticipations I had foreseen Foster and me strolling about on the walks outside, me in my glimmering white sheer dress with the blue underskirt (Mama and I had worked for two weeks on that dress), and Foster with his nice broad aristocratic shoulders. Then, lo and behold, he had worn a white dinner jacket! There was never anybody in creation as proud as I was when I first walked into the senior dance that night with Foster Hamilton.

Pride goeth before a fall. The fall must be the one Foster took down the gully back of the boys' privy at the schoolhouse. I still don't know quite how he did it. When we went outside, he put me carefully in his car, helped to tuck in my skirts, and closed the door in the most polite way, and then I saw him heading toward the privy in his white jacket that was swaying like a lantern through the dark, and then he just wasn't there any more. After a while, I got worried that somebody would come out, like us, for air, so I got out and went to the outside wall of the privy and said, "Foster, are you all right?" I didn't get any answer, so I knocked politely on the wall and said, "Foster?" Then I looked around behind and all around, for I was standing very close to the edge of the gully that had eroded right up to the borders of the campus (somebody was always threatening that the whole schoolhouse was going to cave in into it before another school year went by), and there at the bottom of the gully Foster Hamilton was lying face down, like the slain in battle.

What I should have done, I should have walked right off and left him there till doomsday, or till somebody came along who would use him for a model in a statue to our glorious dead in the defense of Port Claiborne against Gen. Ulysses S. Grant in 1863. That battle was over in about ten minutes, too. But I had to consider how things would look—I had my pride, after all. So I took a look around, hiked up my skirts, and went down into the gully. When I shook Foster, he grunted and rolled over, but I couldn't get him up. I wasn't strong enough. Finally, I said, "Foster, Mama's here!," and he soared up like a Roman candle. I never saw anything like it. He walked straight up the side of the gully and gave me a hand up, too. Then I guided him over toward the car and he sat in the door and lighted a cigarette.

"Where is she?" he said.

"Who?" I said.

"Your mother," he said.

"Oh, I just said that, Foster. I had to get you up someway."

At that, his shoulders slumped down and he looked terribly depressed. "I didn't mean to do this, Marilee," he said. "I didn't have any idea it would hit me this way. I'm sure I'll be all right in a minute."

I don't think he ever did fully realize that he had fallen in the gully. "Get inside," I said, and shoved him over. There were one or two couples beginning to come outside and walk around. I squeezed in beside Foster and closed the door. Inside the gym, where the hot lights were, the music was blaring and beating away. We had got a real orchestra specially for that evening, all the way down from Vicksburg, and a brass-voiced girl was singing a nineteen-thirties song. I would have given anything to be in there with it rather than out in the dark with Foster Hamilton.

I got quite a frisky reputation out of that evening. Disappearing after ten minutes of the dance, seen snuggling out in the car, and gone completely by intermission. I drove us away. Foster wouldn't be convinced that anybody would think it at all peculiar if he reappeared inside the gym with red mud smeared all over his dinner jacket. I didn't know how to drive, but I did anyway. I'm convinced you can do anything when you have to—speak French, do a double back flip off the low diving board, play Rachmaninoff on the piano, or fly an airplane. Well, maybe not fly an airplane; it's too technical. Anyway, that's how I learned to drive a car, riding us up and down the highway, holding off Foster with my elbow, marking time till midnight came and I could go home without anybody thinking anything out of the ordinary had happened.

When I got out of the car, I said, "Foster Hamilton, I never want to see you again as long as I live. And I hope you have a wreck on the way home."

Mama was awake, of course. She called out in the dark, "Did you have a good time, Marilee?"

"Oh, yes, Ma'am," I said.

Then I went back to my shed-ceilinged room in the back wing, and cried and cried. And cried.

There was a good bit of traffic coming and going out to our house after that. A. P. Fortenberry came, all pallid and sober, with a tie on and a straw hat in his hand. Then A. P. and Foster came together. Then Foster came by himself.

The story went that Foster had stopped in the garage with A. P. for a drink before the dance, and instead of water in the drink, A. P. had filled it up with grain alcohol. I was asked to believe that he did this because, seeing Foster all dressed up, he got the idea that Foster was going to some family do, and he couldn't stand Foster's family, they were all so stuckup. While Foster was draining the first glass, A. P. had got called out front to put some gas in a car, and while he was gone Foster took just a little tap more whiskey with another glassful of grain alcohol. A. P. wanted me to understand that Foster's condition that night had been all his fault, that instead of three or four ounces of whiskey, Foster had innocently put down eighteen ounces of sheer dynamite, and it was a miracle only to be surpassed by the resurrection of Jesus Christ that he had managed to drive out and get me, converse with Mama about peach pickle, and dance those famous ten minutes at all.

Well, I said I didn't know. I thought to myself I never heard of Foster Hamilton touching anything he even mistook for water.

All these conferences took place at the front gate. "I never saw a girl like you," Mama said. "Why don't you invite the boys to sit on the porch?"

"I'm not too crazy about A. P. Fortenberry," I said. "I don't think he's a very nice boy."

"Uh-*huh*," Mama said, and couldn't imagine what Foster Hamilton was doing running around with him, if he wasn't a nice boy. Mama, to this day, will not hear a word against Foster Hamilton.

I was still giving some thought to the whole matter that summer, sitting now on the front steps, now on the back steps, and now on the side steps, whichever was most in the shade, chewing on pieces of grass and thinking, when one day the mailman stopped in for a glass of Mama's cold buttermilk (it's famous) and told me that Foster and A. P. had had the most awful wreck. They had been up to Vicksburg, and coming home had collided with a whole carload of Negroes. The carnage was awful—so much blood on everybody you couldn't tell black from white. They were both going to live, though. Being so drunk, which in a way had caused the wreck, had also kept them relaxed enough to come out of it alive. I warned the mailman to leave out the drinking part when he told Mama, she thought Foster was such a nice boy.

The next time I saw Foster, he was out of the hospital

and had a deep scar on his cheekbone like a sunken star. He looked handsomer and more distinguished than ever. I had gotten a scholarship to Millsaps College in Jackson, and was just about to leave. We had a couple of dates before I left, but things were not the same. We would go to the picture show and ride around afterward, having a conversation that went something like this:

"Marilee, why are you such a nice girl? You're about the only nice girl I know."

"I guess I never learned any different, so I can't help it. Will you teach me how to stop being a nice girl?"

"I certainly will not!" He looked to see how I meant it, and for a minute I thought the world was going to turn over; but it didn't.

"Why won't you, Foster?"

"You're too young. And your mama's a real sweet lady. And your daddy's too good a shot."

"Foster, why do you drink so much?"

"Marilee, I'm going to tell you the honest truth. I drink because I like to drink." He spoke with real conviction.

So I went on up to college in Jackson, where I went in for serious studies and made very good grades. Foster, in time, got a job on the paper in New Orleans, where, during off hours, or so I understood, he continued his investigation of the lower things in life and of the effects of alcohol upon the human system.

It is twenty years later now, and Foster Hamilton is down there yet.

Millions of things have happened; the war has come and gone. I live far away, and everything changes, almost every day. You can't even be sure the moon and stars are going to be the same the day after tomorrow night. So it has become more and more important to me to know that Windsor is still right where it always was, standing pure in its decay, and that the gilded hand on the Presbyterian church in Port Claiborne is still pointing to Heaven and not to Outer Space; and I earnestly feel, too, that Foster Hamilton should go right on drinking. There have got to be some things you can count on, would be an ordinary way to put it. I'd rather say that I feel the need of a land, of a sure terrain, of a sort of permanent landscape of the heart.

The Little Brown Girl

Maybeth's father had a business in the town, which was about a mile from where they lived, but he had about forty acres of land below the house that he planted in cotton and corn. The land was down the hill from the house and it was on two levels of ground: twenty acres, then a bluff covered with oak sprouts and vines, then a lower level, which stretched to the property line at the small creek. You could see it all from the house—the two fields and the creek, and other fields beyond the creek—but from the upper field you could just see as far as the willows along the creek bank.

For nine months of the year, Maybeth's father hired a Negro named Jim Williams to make the crop. Jim would work uptown in the mornings and come in the afternoons around two o'clock—a black, strapping Negro in blue overalls, stepping light and free and powerful on the road from town. He would go around the house to the back to hitch up the black mule in spring, or file on the hoe blade in summer, or drag a great dirty-white cotton sack to the field in the fall. Spring, summer, and fall they saw him come, until he became as much a part of the household as Maybeth or Brother or Lester-Junior or Snookums, the cook; then, after the last pound of cotton was weighed in the cold fall twilight, the Jim they knew would vanish. In winter, they sometimes spoke to a town Negro as Jim, and he would answer back, pleasant as you please, but it was no use pretending he was the same. The cotton stalks stood black and sodden in the field, and the cornstalks broke from the top, and there was nothing for a little girl to do in the afternoons but grow all hot and stuffy by the fire or pester Mother for things to eat or study school-books sometimes. There wasn't anybody much to play with out where they lived.

At last, the spring day would come when Maybeth could leap away from the school bus and the ugly children in the bus, and run up the drive to the house, then down the hill, under the maple trees, to the field. Jim would be in the field, plowing with the middlebuster, and she would get to follow behind him for the first time in the year. Jim did a lot of funny things out there in the field. Up ahead, where the rows ended at the top of the bluff, Jim some-times stopped when he had pulled the plow out of the ground, and while the black mule circled in the trace chains he would fling up his head and sing out, rich and full, as loud as he could sing, "Ama-a-zi-in' grace—" The air would quiver for the next line to come, but Jim would be well into the field by then, driving the plow down the furrow with a long, swinging stride.

Once, Maybeth tried to tell him the next line. "It goes 'How sweet the sound,' Jim," she said, trying to put her little shoes in Jim's broad tracks.

But all Jim Williams said was "Git up, Jimson Weed!" Other times, he called the mule Daisy Bell, and that was funny, too, because the mule's name was Dick, and Dick was a man mule. Maybeth was sure he was a man mule. But when she told Jim that, he only said, "Lawd, Lawd," as though she had told him something he had never heard before, or something he had only half heard when she said it. You couldn't tell which.

But most of the time Maybeth was asking Jim questions. When she got like that with Mother, Mother would finally say, "Now, what on earth made you think of that?" Daddy would laugh at her questions and say, "I don't know, honey." But Jim knew the answer to everything. He knew why the jaybird bounced on the air when he flew and why the mule swept his nose along the ground when he turned and why the steel plow slid out of the earth as clean as when it entered. Sometimes Maybeth knew that Jim was making up, but most of the time she believed him word for word, like the catechism in Sunday school.

One spring afternoon, a few days before Maybeth's seventh birthday, Jim was sporting a new red bandanna in the back pocket of his overalls. Even before Maybeth reached him, she spotted it, and she asked about it first thing.

"My little girl give me that," he said. He spoke in his making-up voice, but he looked perfectly straight-faced.

Maybeth hurried very fast behind him. "Aw, Jim, you ain't got a little girl, have you? How old is she?"

"She be eight nex' fall," he said, very businesslike. "Gee, mule."

"How big is she?"

"She jes' 'bout your size, honey."

A little brown girl in a starched blue-and-white checked

dress stepped smiling before Maybeth's eyes. From then on, Maybeth's questions all went in one direction, and if Jim had any peace, it was only because he was Jim.

"When will I get to see her, Jim? When will she come and play with me?"

"Some day nex' week, I reckon."

"What day next week?"

"Long 'bout the middle part of the week, I spec'."

"Aw, you're just foolin', Jim. Aren't you just foolin'?"

"Ama-a-zi-in' grace—" sang Jim Williams as the black mule turned in the trace chains against a low and burning cloud. And that night, when Jim had eaten his supper in the kitchen and gone, the little brown girl in the blue-and-white checked dress stayed on.

"Mother, guess what Jim told me today," said Maybeth, opening her arithmetic book before the fire. "He said he had a little girl. She's coming and play with me."

"Oh, honey, Jim's just fooling you. Jim hasn't got any children, has he, Lester?"

"Not that I ever heard of," said Daddy. "It's a good thing, too—the way he drinks and carries on every Saturday night."

"He's fooling you," said Mother.

Maybeth bent quickly to her sums. "I know it," she said.

And in a way she had known it all along. But in another way she hadn't known it, and the not knowing still remained along with the knowing, and she never thought it out any further. Nothing was changed, and she and the little brown girl played together before she went to sleep at night, in dull moments at school, and when she was

being quiet on the bus, riding home with the noisy children. The little girl was the first thing to ask questions
about when she ran to the field after school, the warm sun
on her yellow hair, and her feet already uncomfortable to
be out of their shoes.

The first thing, that is, until the Friday came when
Maybeth was seven. It was a perfect birthday. Under her
plate at breakfast that morning she found two broad silver
dollars. The class sang "Happy Birthday" to her in school,
and that night Snookums, the cook, who usually finished
work in the afternoon, returned from her house to cook
supper, and they all had fried chicken and rice and gravy
and a coconut birthday cake.

Maybeth ran into the kitchen to show her silver dollars
to Snookums and Jim. "Look, Snookums! Look, Jim!" she
said.

"Lawd-ee!" said Snookums. She was a young, bright
Negro with a slim waist and straight black hair.

"My, *my!*" said Jim. "That's ringin' money, ain't it,
Snookum?"

"Lawd-ee!" said Snookums.

"Which you druther have, Snookum," said Jim, "ringin'
money or foldin' money?"

The door was open to the dining room, and Maybeth
heard her big brother laugh and holler back, "Either one'll
do to buy Saturday-night liquor, won't it?"

Jim and Snookums just fell out laughing, and Maybeth
somehow felt ashamed.

After supper, she put the two silver dollars in a little
box inside a bigger box and put them in the very back
right-hand corner of her drawer in the bureau.

The next day was Saturday, and it rained, so Jim stayed in the barn and shelled corn for the chickens, and Maybeth watched.

"I *wuz* gwine bring my little girl to play with you nex' week," said Jim.

Maybeth was stricken. "How come you can't, Jim? Oh, how come you can't?"

"She ain't got no fine dress like you is. She ain't got nothin' 'cept one ole brown dress. She say she shame to come."

Maybeth broke the stubborn grains of corn from a cob one at a time, and her heart beat very fast. "Have you sure 'nough got a little girl, Jim?"

Jim did not answer. "There's dresses at the Jew store," he went on mournfully. "But they's nigh onto two dollars. Take the nigger long time to make up that money."

A few minutes later, Maybeth was hurrying back to the house in the rain.

She took the two silver dollars out of the little box within the larger box, and ran back to the barn.

"What you fixin' to do?" Jim Williams asked, holding the two coins in his open palm and cutting his eyes toward her.

"For the dress," Maybeth said. "You know. For your little girl's dress, Jim."

"Your daddy ain't gwine like you playing around with this money," he said.

"He ain't going to know," said Maybeth.

"You *sure?*" he asked, snapping shut the three clasps on his little leather purse.

"I'm not going to tell him," said Maybeth.

"Gwine git her a yalla dre-ess," sang Jim softly, and the corn poured out of his fingers in rich handfuls and rattled against the side of the scuttle as fast as the rain on the tin roof.

Maybeth did not know why she had given Jim the money. It was like when you are playing mud pies by yourself and you get real salt and pepper for the pies, or when you are dressing up to play lady and you make a mess of all the closets and cedar chests trying to get something real and exactly right—the high-heeled button shoes or the hat with the plume. She and Jim were playing that Jim had a little girl. But when the playing was over, Jim did not give the money back, and, of course, she did not really know that she had expected him to, so she never asked. And because she wasn't exactly sure what money meant, her sorrow centered on the two little empty boxes in the corner of the dresser drawer.

She thought of them with an empty feeling when she rode to school on Monday morning in the pickup with Daddy and saw a yellow dress in the Jew-store window. When she rode back from school on the bus, she looked again, and something went queer inside her, because the yellow dress was gone.

Maybeth ran so hard down the hill to the field that afternoon that the pound of her feet shook her all over and she could hardly stop running at the fence. All the way home in the bus, all the way through the yard and down the hill, she could picture Jim plowing with the little girl in the yellow dress behind him in the furrow, and they would look up when Maybeth came. From the fence, she could see that Jim was plowing down at the far corner, where the land was lowest; he was almost through busting the upper field. She could just see the top of his head following Dick's flapping ears up the slope. Maybeth crawled through the barbed wire and caught a snag in her dress. When she had pulled it free, and looked up, Jim was in full view on the higher ground, and he was alone.

Maybeth came slowly out of the maple shade into the hot sun. As she crossed the rows, the clods made her stumble once or twice. She fell in behind him at last.

"I tore my dress. See?" she said, holding up the snagged hem.

He glanced back, the sweat big on his temples and catching the sun on his cheek. "Sho' did," he said. "You shorely did."

They were back beside the bluff before she asked, "How come your little girl didn't come today, Jim?"

He had stopped, with the plow in the new furrow, to cut himself a plug of tobacco. He jerked his kinky head toward the creek. "She down there," he said.

"Down there?"

"She shame to come till you come. She say she gwine set in the bushes and watch for you. She be comin' on in a minute now."

Maybeth ran to the edge of the bluff, among the honeysuckle vines, and stared and stared down toward the low willows along the creek bank, until their sharp spring green blurred in her eyes.

"Where, Jim, where?"

Jim hooked the lines over the plow handle. "Whoa, mule," he said. He walked away from her along the edge of the bluff and stood on the highest point, bigger than anything from sky to sky. He pointed.

"See," he said, and his tone was infinite. "Look yonder. She setting on the groun'. See. She done crossed her legs."

"Has she got on a—a yellow dress?"

"Yes'm! Yes'm! You sees her! You sees her sho'!"

"Is she sitting under that bigges' clump of willow, right over yonder? Sitting cross-legged?"

"Yes'm! That's right! By that bigges' clump."

"Sort of with one hand on the ground?"

"Yes, Ma'am! You sees her sho'!"

Then, in two strides, he was back at the plow. "She'll come. My little girl'll come. Gee, mule. She knows we done seen her, and she'll come. Gee up, sir!"

The plow ran into the earth, and Maybeth, still standing on the bluff, could hear from somewhere the creak of the harness, and the tearing of little roots as the soft ground was severed. She stood staring, and the green blur beyond the lower field fanned out and then closed together around the shape of something—was it something?—like a still image under the willow trees. Humming to himself, Jim Williams passed farther down the slope, but Maybeth stayed on the bluff, as motionless as the fluted honeysuckle bloom beside her hand and the willows across the lower field standing up in the windless air.

She saw something move under the willows.

Maybeth began to walk, and then she began to run, faster and faster. The rows, with their heavy chunks of clodded earth, flew beneath her, trying to trip her, to keep her from the hill and the white house on the hill and Mother.

She caught her breath a little in the yard, and then she went in and found Mother in the kitchen, drinking some water.

"Why, precious, why are you so hot?" Mother said. "Why did you come back from the field?"

How could you tell about the yellow dress and something coming alive beneath the willows? "I—I got hungry," said Maybeth.

Mother gave her a piece of cold corn bread and sent her out on the back steps. There was a sound around the corner of the house. A Bantam rooster stepped toward her on the flagstone walk. Maybeth jumped up, trembling, and flung the muffin to him and ran into the house, through one room and another.

"Mother!" she called. "Mother!"

"In here, honey."

When she came into the room, her mother looked up at her. Then she laid aside her darning basket and took Maybeth into her arms and rocked her in the rocking chair.

The Day Before

When I started to school, my grandfather and the old maid next door and her two old bachelor brothers took a great interest in the event, so important in my life, and tried to do everything they could think of for me. One bought me a lunch basket; another planned just what should be put in it, and Miss Charlene Thomas, the old maid, made me a book satchel out of green linen with my initial embroidered on it in gold thread. Somebody even went uptown to the drugstore where the school books were sold and got me a new primer to replace an old one, still perfectly good, which had belonged to my cousin. And there was a pencil box, also green, with gilt lettering saying *PENCILS*, containing: three long yellow Ticonderoga pencils, an eraser—one end for ink, the other for lead—a pen staff, two nibs, and a tiny steel pencil sharpener. My grandfather laid the oblong box across his knees, unsnapped the cover, and carefully using the sharpener he began to sharpen the pencils. After doing one of them and dusting off his trousers, he took out his pen knife, which had a bone handle, and sharpened the other two in the manner which he preferred. Then he closed up the box and handed it to me. I put it in the satchel along with the primer.

Mr. Dave Thomas, one of the two bachelor brothers of Miss Charlene, having made a special trip uptown in the August heat, came in to say that copy books were not yet on sale as they had not arrived, but could be bought for a nickel from the teachers on opening day. "Here's a nickel right now," said Mr. Dave, digging in his trousers' pocket. "*I'll* give her one," said my grandfather. I was spoiled to death, but I did not know it. Miss Charlene was baking ginger cakes to go in my lunch basket. I went around saying that I hated to go to school because I would have to put shoes on, but everybody including the cook laughed at such a flagrant lie. I had been dying to start to school for over a year.

My grandfather said that the entire family was smart and that I would make good grades, too. My mother said she did not think I would have any trouble the first year because I already knew how to read a little (I had, in fact, already read through the primer). "After that, I don't know," she said. I wondered if she meant that I would fail the second grade. This did not fill me with any alarm, any more than hearing that somebody had died, but made me feel rather cautious. Mr. Ed, Mr. Dave's brother, called me all the way over across the calf lot to his house to show me how to open a new book. I stood by his chair, one bare foot on top the other, watching him while he spread the pages out flat, first from the center, then taking up a few at a time on either side and smoothing them out in a steady firm way, slowly, so as not to crack the spine, and so on until all were done. It was a matter, he said (so they all said), of having respect for books. He said that I should do it a second time, now that he had showed me how. "Make sure your hands are clean," he said, "then we can go eat some cold watermelon." I remember still the smell of that particular book, the new pages, the binding, the glue, and the print as combining to make a book smell—a particular thing. The pencil box had another smell altogether, as did the new linen of the satchel. My brown shoes were new also, a brand called Buster Brown. I did not like the name, for it was invariably printed above a picture of a little round-faced boy with straight bangs and square-cut hair who was smiling as though he was never anything but cheerful. I did not know what I looked like especially, but I knew I did not look like that, nor did I want to. I asked to be allowed to wear new tennis shoes to school, and if not new ones, then old ones. My mother said I could not wear tennis shoes of any description to school and when I said I wanted to go barefoot then, she said I was crazy. I told my grandfather but he only said I had to mind her. I felt that he would have let me do as I liked and was only saying what he had to. I felt that my parents were never as intelligent as my grandfather, Mr. Dave, Mr. Ed, and Miss Charlene.

After dinner that day it was very hot and when everybody lay down and quit fanning themselves with funeral parlor fans because they had fallen sound asleep, some with the fans laid across their chests or stomachs and some snoring, the two Airedales that belonged to Mr. Dave had running fits. If a relative was visiting, or any stranger to our road, which was a street that didn't go anywhere except to us and the Thomas house, they were liable to get

scared to death by those Airedales because the way they
sometimes tore around in hot weather it looked as if they
had gone mad. It was something about the heat that
affected their brains and made them start running. It all
happened silently; they would just come boiling out of nowhere, frothing at the mouth, going like two balls of fire,
first around Miss Charlene's house, then up and down the
calf lot between their house and ours, then all around our
house, finally tearing out toward the field in front of the
house, where, down among the cotton and the corn, they
would wear it all out like the tail of a tornado. Eventually
the foliage would stop shaking and after a long while they
would come dragging themselves out again, heads down
and tongues lolling, going back to where they belonged.
They would crawl under the house and sleep for hours.
We had got used to their acting this way, and though it
was best, we agreed, to keep out of their way, they did
not scare us. The Negro children used to watch them
more closely than anybody did, saying "Hoo, boy, look
a-yonder." White people had sunstrokes or heat strokes or
heat exhaustion—I did not ever learn quite what the difference in these conditions was, and don't know yet. Dogs
had running fits instead.

The Airedales were named Pet and Beauty, and only
Mr. Dave, who owned them, could tell them apart. He
took their fits as being a sort of illness, and as he loved
them, he worried about them. He gave them buttermilk
out of dishes on the floor and got them to take cobalt blue
medicine out of a spoon, holding their jaws wide with his
thumb, pouring in the medicine, then clamping the jaws
shut tight. It must have tasted awful, for the dogs always

resisted swallowing and tried to fight free, their paws clawing the ground, head lashing around to get away and eyes rolling white and terrible. They could jump straight up and fight like wild ponies, but he always brought them down, holding on like a vise and finally, just when it seemed they weren't ever going to, they would give up and swallow. Then it was all over. I never knew if the medicine did them any good or not.

They had one of their fits that very afternoon, the day before school started. We had a friend of my aunt's from out in the country who had stopped by and been persuaded to stay for dinner and she saw them out her window and woke everybody up out of their nap. "Those dogs!" she cried. "Just look at those dogs!" "It's all right!" my father hollered from down the hall. "They've just got running fits, Miss Fannie," my mother cried. "It's not rabies," she added. "At least they don't bark," said my grandfather, who was angry because she had waked him up. He didn't care much for her anyway and said she had Indian blood.

I don't know what I thought school was going to be like. It was right up the road, only about twenty minutes' walk, just a little too far to come home for dinner, and I had passed the building and campus all my life, since I could remember. My brother had gone there, and all my cousins, and still were recognizable when they returned home from it. But to me, in my imagination beforehand, it was a blur, in the atmosphere of which my mind faltered, went blank, and came to with no clear picture whatsoever.

After I got there it was all clear enough, but strange to

the last degree. I might as well have been in another state or even among Yankees, whom I had heard about but never seen. I could see our house from the edge of the campus, but it seemed to me I was observing it from the moon. There were many children there, playing on the see-saws, sliding down the sliding board, drinking at the water fountains, talking and running and lining up to file inside to the classrooms. All of them seemed to know each other. I myself did not recognize any of them except occasionally one of the older ones who went to our tiny Sunday School. They stopped and said, "Hey," and I said, "Hey." One said, "I didn't know you were starting to school." And I said, "Yes I am." I went up to a child in my grade and said that I lived down that street there and pointed. "I know it," she answered. She had white-blonde hair, pale blue eyes and very fair skin, and did not look at me when she spoke. The way she said "I know it" gave me to understand that she probably knew just about everything. I have seen sophisticated people since, and at that time I did not, of course, know the word, but she was, and always remained in my mind, its definition. I did not want to go away and stand by myself again, so I said, "I live next door to Miss Charlene Thomas and Mr. Dave and Mr. Ed Thomas." "I know it," she said again, still not looking at me. After a time she said, "They feed their old dogs out of Havilland china." It was my turn to say I know it, because I certainly had seen it happen often enough. But I said nothing at all.

I had often lingered for long minutes before the glass-front china cabinet on its tiny carved bowed legs, the glass, not flat, but swelling smoothly forward like a sheet in the wind, and marvelled to see all the odd-shaped matching dishes—"Syllabub cups," Miss Charlene said, when I asked her. "Bone dishes," she said, "for when you eat fish." There were tiny cups and large cups, sauce bowls and gravy boats, and even a set of salt holders, no bigger than a man's thumb, each as carefully painted as a platter. It was known to me that this china, like the house itself and all the fine things in it, the rosewood my mother admired, the rose taffeta draperies and gilt mirrors, had belonged to the aunt of the three Thomases, a certain Miss Bedford, dead before I was born, who had been highly educated, brilliant in conversation, and whose parrot could quote Shakespeare. I did not find the words to tell any of this to the girl who knew everything. The reason I did not was because, no more than I knew how to do what she so easily accomplished in regard to the dogs' being fed out of Havilland china—which had often been held up to the light for me and shown to be transparent as an eggshell—I did not know what value to give to what I knew, what my ears had heard, eyes had seen, hands had handled, nor was there anything I could say about it. I did not think the child was what my grandfather meant by being smart, but I did know that she made me feel dumb. I retreated and was alone again, but a day is a long time when you are six and you cannot sit opening and closing your new pencil box forever. So I went up to other children and things of the same sort continued to happen. In the classroom I did as I was told, and it was easy. I must have realized by the end of the week that I would never fail the second or any other grade. So everything would be all right.

From then on, life changed in a certain way I could not

define, and at home in the afternoons and on weekends I did not feel the same. I missed something but did not know what it was. I knew if I lived to be a thousand I would never do anything but accept it if an old man fed his dogs out of the best china or if a parrot could quote Shakespeare. At home when I looked up, I saw the same faces; even the dogs were the same, named the same, though they, as was usual, had stopped having fits once the nights got cooler. Everybody, every single person, was just the same. Yet I was losing them; they were fading before my eyes. You can go somewhere, anywhere you want—any day now you can go to the moon—but you can't ever quite come back. Having gone up a road and entered a building at an appointed hour, there was no way to come back out of it and feel the same about my grand-father, ginger cakes, or a new book satchel. This was the big surprise, and I had no power over it.

Life is important right down to the last crevice and corner. The tumult of a tree limb against the stormy early morning February sky will tell you forever about the poetry, the tough non-sad, non-guilty struggle of nature. It is important the way ants go one behind the other, hurrying to get there, up and down the white-painted front-porch post. The nasty flash and crack of lightning, striking a tall young tree, is something you have got to see to know about. Nothing can change it; it is just itself.

So nothing changed, nothing and nobody, and yet hav-ing once started to lose them a little, I couldn't make the stream run backward, I lost them completely in the end. The little guilt, the little sadness I felt sometimes: was it because I hadn't really wanted them enough, held on tightly enough, had not, in other words, loved them?

They are, by now, nearly every one dead and buried—dogs, parrot, people, and all. The furniture was all either given away or inherited by cousins from far away, the house bought by somebody and chopped up into apartments; none of this can really be dwelt on or thought of as grievous: that is an easy way out.

For long before anybody died, or any animal, I was walking in a separate world; our questions and answers, visits and exchanges no more communicated what they had once than if we were already spirits and flesh and could walk right through each other without knowing it.

Years later, only a few months ago, when home for a visit, I was invited to play bridge with some friends and on the coffee table saw a box of blue milk glass, carved with a golden dragon across the lid, quite beautiful. "That came out of the old Thomas house," my friend said. She had got it in a devious way, which she related, but had never been able to open it. I picked it up, not remembering it, and without even thinking my finger moved at once to the hidden catch, and the box flew open. It wasn't chance; I must have once been shown how it worked, and something in me was keeping an instinctive faith with what it knew. Had they never been lost then at all? I wondered. A great hidden world shimmered for a moment, grew almost visible, just beyond the breaking point of knowledge. Had nothing perhaps ever been lost by that great silent guardian within?

About the Author

Elizabeth Spencer was born in Carrollton, Mississippi, in 1921 and has been writing fiction since early childhood. After graduation from Belhaven College in 1942, she took an M.A. in English at Vanderbilt University the following year. For the next two years she taught English in Mississippi and at a school for girls in Nashville, then became a reporter for the *Nashville Tennessean*.

Miss Spencer's first novel, *Fire in the Morning*, was published in 1948, and was declared by *The New York Times Book Review* one of the three best first novels of that year. Her second, *This Crooked Way*, appeared in 1952, while she was teaching creative writing at the University of Mississippi. In 1953 the author received a Guggenheim Fellowship and went to Italy for two years, living principally in Florence and Rome. Her third novel, *The Voice at the Back Door*, 1956, received notable critical success, including the Rosenthal Award of the National Institute of Arts and Letters, and the Kenyon Review Fiction Fellowship. *The Voice at the Back Door* was followed by Miss Spencer's renowned novel, *The Light in the Piazza*, in 1960, and *Knights and Dragons*, published in 1965. *No Place for an Angel*, published in 1967 to distinguished reviews, further enhanced Miss Spencer's reputation as one of the major American writers of fiction and considerably enlarged her audience.

Elizabeth Spencer's stories, known for their subtlety and simplicity, appear frequently in *The New Yorker* and other magazines. She is married to John Rusher of Cornwall, England, and they now live near Montreal.

40